GRACE DESIGNS MYSTERIES

BACKSTITCHED AND STABBED

TILLY WALLACE

Print ISBN: 978-1-7385845-5-0

v01082023

Cover design by Melody Simmons

Editing Kat's Literary Services

To be the first to hear about Tilly's new releases and exclusive offers, sign up at:

https://www.tillywallace.com/newsletter

Blurb

BACKSTITCHED AND STABBED

The only thing worse than wet woollen togs is a knife in the back...

As the Kiwi summer draws to a close, a family outing to the beach takes a deadly turn when a lifeless body washes up on shore. Grace is devastated to recognise the victim, Ricky, who worked in her friend's bakery. But when the supposed drowning victim is rolled over, a shocking truth is revealed—he was murdered.

Drawn into finding the murderer of the cheerful baker, Grace picks at the tangled web of secrets that surrounded Ricky. The man lived a double, or even triple, life. But which version of him had provoked the fatal encounter? Grace and her friends must find the person responsible before another life is lost to the same tide of violence that claimed Ricky.

The second instalment in the Grace Designs mystery series, about a seamstress turned sleuth in Wellington, New Zealand at the dawn of the 1920s.

Chapter One

SATURDAY, 28 February 1920.

"If you don't hold still, we will miss the ferry." I swear that the ability of a small child to hold still, is inversely related to how much time you have.

Theo, my son, had inherited his father's pale skin and as a consequence, burned easily. As he squirmed to rush for the motorcar waiting to take us to the wharf, I was trying to ensure his hat was tightly wedged on his head and the string tied securely under his chin. In the end, I won. But only because Dad blocked the door and pointed to the hat on his head. If Grandpa wore one to the beach, apparently it was acceptable.

Outside in the narrow lane, Joseph sat at the wheel of a large travelling vehicle. For a moment, I wondered how he had manoeuvred it there, but it spoke to his skill that he most likely reversed up around the corner to get it into place. The vehicle was kindly loaned to us for the short trip by my mentor, Mrs Cooper, on the condition that Joseph helps her driver wash it afterwards. My cousin had moments of lingering guilt after recent events, even though I reassured him there was no bad blood between us. He had an intense loyalty to his job as a police officer and Detective Archer, but I had smudged the edges.

They say you can't beat Wellington on a good day, and today was a top one. The gusty winds had dropped, the sky didn't have a cloud for miles, and despite the early hour, the warmth promised that the last day of summer would be a scorcher. Determined to take advantage of the predicted glorious weekend, we decided yesterday to head to Days Bay for a picnic. Situated across the harbour, the beach was a popular spot for Wellingtonians wanting to relax, go for a swim, or build a sandcastle.

Sam and her mother joined us and we had an assortment of baskets containing our swimsuits, towels, books, toys to entertain Theo, and most importantly... our lunch. As a point of honour, the Kostas women brought enough food with them to feed a family of twenty, not the five of us. The only things we lacked were chairs and an umbrella, but we would hire those when we reached our destination.

Dad gripped the handle of his cane, and I slipped my arm through his as Theo raced to leap into the open-top motorcar.

"Foot giving you some pain?" I asked as we stepped outside.

He locked the door and gave me a lopsided grin. "Damn toes are itchy. I'm looking forward to a paddle in the ocean. That'll satisfy them."

Dad suffered with pains in the missing limb, which seemed unfair to me. How could an appendage that was no longer attached feel anything? Yet I had heard of returned soldiers who experienced the same phenomenon. For Dad, the only thing that relieved the symptoms was immersing the phantom foot in the salty water. At times, I wondered if my father was part sea creature, such was his love of the ocean and his need to be near it.

A short ride later, Joseph dropped us close to the wharf. Sadly, it seemed most of Wellington had the same idea as us, and we were all crammed onto the wharf to catch the steamer across the water. I kept a tight grip on Theo's hand, not wanting to lose him in the crowd. The four adults formed a tight cluster with Theo in the middle, which meant his view of events was restricted to waistbands and bottoms.

Thankfully, we didn't have to wait too long before the crowd surged forward to pile onto the *Duchess*. The steamer could hold over 1,000 passengers, and I was convinced there were at least that many, if not more, all seeking to enjoy the last days of summer. Dad and I insisted on sitting up on deck, which made Sam grumble.

"It's all right for you Sullivans with salt in your

veins. Some of us were born to stay on land," she muttered as she sat with her back to the water.

"You're half-Greek, and your dad grew up in a fishing village." I nudged her.

"I inherited mum's land-loving traits." Sam was smartly dressed in pale linen trousers, a white short-sleeved shirt, and a straw boater. She would have looked at home lounging on an expensive yacht sailing the Mediterranean Sea.

"Would you rather be wedged in the cabin with sweaty land lubbers who vomit at the slightest wave?" We Sullivans were exhilarated by rough waves. The action of the ocean made us come alive.

Sam grimaced at the idea of the smelly interior below. "Perhaps not."

Theo clung to the rail to watch the water race past the hull and laughed when spray dotted across his face. I closed my eyes, enjoying the gentle up and down motion of the steamer that made others rush to the rail for quite a different reason than enjoyment.

As I basked in the moment, a pressing situation tapped for my attention. In the rush of getting out the door, my motherly instincts made sure Theo had been to the toilet, but I completely forgot about my own needs.

"I need to go to the bathroom," I whispered to Sam before getting to my feet. There would still be three sets of eyes to keep track of Theo.

The narrow stairs took me below deck and to the tiny bathroom cubicles. The rank odour of sweat permeated the stuffy air. Polite smiles were exchanged among those waiting, but thankfully it wasn't too long before it was my turn. The oiled wooden door opened and a familiar face stepped out, Ricky Hammond. The young man worked in the Kostas Bakery. He appeared to be suffering from a touch of seasickness, with a sheen to his face and a slight green undertone to his skin.

"Hello, Ricky," I called out as he held the door open.

"Mrs Devine." His eyes widened until they seemed all black pupils. "I have wanted to ask you, don't you have a relative in the police?"

"Oh, yes. Joseph, my cousin, is a constable." What an odd question.

"There's a queue, you know!" someone yelled out from behind us.

"I'll find you later," he murmured.

With an apologetic smile at having to cut the small talk short, I reached out to grab the door as the ship hit a wave and rolled to starboard.

Ricky flung out an arm to steady himself, his bare skin grazing across mine.

I hurried to step into the toilet and slam the door as a transferred memory leapt up my arm and burst into my mind.

'You don't betray your team,' he spat out in short, angry syllables. A stubby finger attached to a meaty hand pointed in my face with each one.

Sweat beaded between my shoulder blades and fear trickled down my spine. I licked my lips but my mouth was so dry, there was no relief to be had. How did he know? 'Teams change. Some players retire. Others move to different games.'

'No one leaves unless I let you. Remember what we do to traitors.'

It took several breaths to shake off the memory. There was only one thing that *you don't betray your team* could mean and that might press on the young man's mind. Given the New Zealand obsession with rugby, he had probably backed the provincial Manawatu team over the Wellington Lions. Or, horror, perhaps Ricky was part Australian and dared to back their team over the Invincibles.

Someone banged on the door. "Are you all right in there?" an older male voice asked.

How rude to interrupt someone while on the loo. My business taken care of, I hurried out.

"So sorry," I murmured to the grumpy man looming over the door as though he guarded it to ensure he was next.

Back up on deck, I dropped beside Sam. The bay was visible already and soon the steamer would slow for its approach. Then we would be packed like sardines for the walk along the jetty. "I saw Ricky below."

"I don't keep him chained by the oven like Cinderella. He's allowed time off." She had one hand on her hat, not relying on the tightness of the band to keep it secure on her head.

"He didn't look well." The memory would stay

tucked inside me for now. Out on the open deck, anyone could hear our conversation, and I wanted time to mull over what it meant. Most probably nothing. But usually, the memories that thrust themselves into me meant the other person was in some sort of pickle, and I was supposed to do something about it. Later, when Theo was playing in the sand and Dad was snoozing with an open book on his chest, I would seek Sam's opinion about what I saw.

It didn't take too long before the steamer sounded its horn to alert everyone to our imminent arrival. Although how anyone could be curled up inside and miss our journey, I didn't know. We waited for the bulk of people to rush for the exit before we picked up our baskets. Dad leaned heavily on his cane today, as we walked along the salt-laden timbers of the wharf at a slow pace. Excitable children surged past us, and Theo gave them a longing look and tugged on my hand.

"It's rude to run off and leave Poppa behind, Theo," I reminded him.

He shot me a look that was part-apologetic and part-pure longing. It took another thirty seconds to reach the end of the jetty, a lifetime to an impatient four-year-old. Following Dad's directions, we staked out our spot on the sand near a stand of trees. We weren't too far from the Pavilion, but what Theo considered a *dumb distance* from the water.

Dad chuckled and pointed to the people spreading blankets and digging umbrellas into the sand only ten feet from the water's edge. "The tide is coming in,

Theo. You wait, by lunchtime we'll have the best spot and all those poor sods will be dragging everything up to the grass."

Sam and I walked up to the Pavilion while Dad and Mrs Kostas spread out our blankets and set the baskets to weigh down the corners. We hired two deck chairs and a large striped umbrella and carried them back to our spot. Then we took turns to use the changing rooms. I was very excited to show off my new swimsuit. Made of navy wool with a smart white trim, it had shorts that stopped above my knee and an overdress on top. Fashion dictated stockings and swimming shoes as well, but in this case, I decided to be practical. It was simply too warm and I wanted to bury my bare toes in the golden sand.

"You rebel. I'll have you wearing trousers every day, yet," Sam said as we exited the busy shed.

She wore a similar outfit to mine but in red. The men's costume was far too scandalous, even for my brave friend. Neither of us wore soft-soled swimming shoes, and I let out a sigh as heated sand flicked over my toes.

Dad modelled a woollen one-piece in wide grey and white horizontal stripes that I had made for him.

"Can I go for a swim, Mum?" Theo wheedled. He wore a swimsuit of the same grey stripe as Dad, although with a smaller torso, his had far fewer stripes!

"I'll stay here and guard lunch." Mrs Kostas settled in the deckchair and under the shade of the umbrella.

"Are you sure Mum, you'd normally love a swim?" Sam asked her mother.

"Later, love. I have a book I want to finish first." She patted the large tome on her lap.

"Come on then, Theo." Taking his hand (regardless of how he stuck his lip out), we strolled through the crowd of cheerful people to the water's edge.

Dad hopped beside us, having left both his wooden foot and cane behind. He could use his stump to balance (having lost the foot at the ankle) but it gave him a lopsided gait like a boat being tossed in a heavy sea.

Worry gnawed at me, wondering if he would be all right, but I'd never insult him by saying that out loud. Instead, I asked, "Off for a swim?"

"Of course." Dad grinned and ambled out deeper. His odd gait unnoticeable once the water submerged his stump and took his weight for him. Half-selkie that he was, he soon dived under a wave and with a few powerful strokes, he headed out to deeper water.

"I wish I could swim like Poppa." Theo tugged me out into the water.

"Listen during your lessons, instead of holding your breath to sit at the bottom of the pool, and you soon will." I tried to appear stern, but it was difficult. The teacher nearly had a heart attack the first time he did a head count and came up one short. Theo had sat clutching his knees on the bottom of the pool. That child could hold his breath for a long time. As I discovered during some impressive tantrums he threw as a two-year-old.

Once he had given his solemn promise not to go past his little knees, I agreed to let go of his hand. Soon, a couple of friends joined him, and the boys splashed each other and ran back and forth in front of watchful mothers.

Sam stood beside me and we chatted while Theo played. Another familiar face walked past.

"Two of my favourite girls!" Harry stopped in front of us. His wiry physique was displayed in a blue and yellow striped costume. His eyes were hidden behind dark sunglasses and a straw hat shaded his face.

"Hello, you," Sam said.

Seeing Harry reminded me of who else I saw earlier. "I saw Ricky on the steamer. Are you lads out for a day in the sun?"

Harry's wide smile dropped away. "We boarded the steamer together. But I fear he suffered cold feet when he realised the other lads weren't coming with us. I shall track him down later. He simply must see how magnificent I look in this outfit."

"He probably spotted someone else he knows and stopped for a chat." It only took a matter of minutes for Theo to find school chums among the beachgoers, and I doubt age changed that ability. A personable lad like Ricky probably encountered many friends between water and sand.

"Why don't you join us for lunch? We have plenty

of food, and he might be more comfortable in a group he knows." Sam gestured back to where her mother sat.

"Will do." Harry saluted and then waded out.

"Expecting Ricky to spend his day off with his employer?" I nudged Sam with my elbow.

"I'm not a monster and can carry a conversation on a wide range of topics I'll have you know." Sam huffed, but it was all bluff. Under her tough skin, she hid the softest heart.

Time flowed with the ebb of the tide and before we knew it, mothers called to children and summoned them to lunch. I reclaimed Theo and as we settled on the blanket, Dad emerged from the water and hobbled back up to our spot. He briskly rubbed off the salt water with his towel, then dropped into the deckchair.

Harry joined us. Alone.

Sam raised an eyebrow, and we shared a look. Poor chap. It looked like his romance was doomed before it left the starting block.

Chapter Two

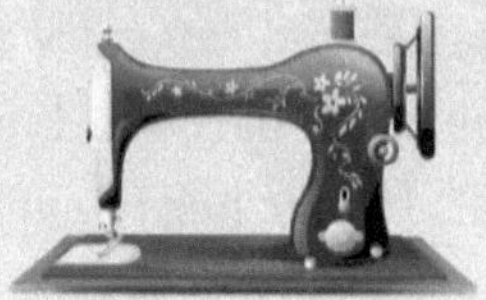

"Sandwich?" Mrs Kostas held a plate with a selection of crustless club sandwiches under Harry's nose.

We'd soon have his heartache submerged by heartburn with the number of cakes and sweet treats we could shovel down him. I hadn't spent a lot of time in Harry's company and enjoyed his conversation over lunch. While he worked as a librarian at Victoria University, he had a critical eye for fashion and kept up a biting critique of the women around us.

"Can I have a donkey ride, please?" Theo pointed with a sticky finger at the animal walking back and forth.

"Of course. But finish your lunch first." The donkeys had the tolerance of saints, as excited children bounced in the saddle and handlers trod the same path back and forth across the beach.

We chatted and laughed and ate until we were all as stuffed as after Christmas dinner. Over at the Pavilion, musicians played from the deep verandah and people gathered to listen and sing the words to songs they knew. Theo had his much longed-for donkey ride, only to complain that the creature was too slow and he much preferred the leggy hacks on his uncle's farm. My mothering instinct had a slight moment of panic at his need for speed, and I imagined him charging around the roads on the bicycle I had bought him for his birthday.

Then another vision rose before my eyes of an adult Theo wearing goggles as he zoomed around a racetrack at unimaginable speeds. A shudder worked its way through my body. I might encourage him towards safer occupations, like woodwork. Although even that came with dangers from saws and machinery.

My gaze softened, and my shoulders relaxed. A mother simply couldn't protect her child from every danger or hazard in the world. No matter how much she wanted to. I would have to find a way to keep my concerns locked inside my heart and allow my son to stretch his wings and make mistakes.

"How about an ice cream?" I asked as we walked back to Dad.

Theo grinned with wide eyes, and the cleft in his chin dimpled. "Oh, yes! Might I have strawberry, please?"

"I'll help you carry them." Sam brushed sand from her knees and joined me.

The wooden Pavilion had been built in the previous century and was a confection of gables, fretwork, and iron finials marching across the roof. Within the sprawling structure was a restaurant and enough room for evening dances. They even hosted outdoor concerts, similar to today's performance.

We lined up to purchase ice creams and from our shady spot, the queue gave me time to stare inside the restaurant. My eyes gobbled up bright patterns and the cut of summer dresses with the eagerness with which my son would devour his icy treat. A clang followed by a tinkle drew my attention to one linen-draped table.

A waiter with his back to me held the stem of a broken glass in one hand, a silver tray in the other. It seemed the full glass did not survive the trip to the table.

"Don't just stand there, you oaf! Clean up this mess!" A tall and narrow blond man at the table pushed his chair back, as a trickle of red wine flowed over the table cloth leaving a dark cherry rivulet. "And bring me another glass immediately."

"Yes, sir. I'm so sorry, sir," the waiter murmured. He dropped pieces of glass to the tray while another waiter rushed to assist and dabbed at the tablecloth. Then a third arrived on the scene with fresh linen. How many staff would converge on the table?

"What flavours, miss?" another voice cut through the drama unfolding in the dining room.

"Oh, one strawberry and two chocolate, please," I answered for my family while Sam picked for her and her mum.

The attendant scooped ice cream from the metal

containers kept inside the ice chest and placed the orbs into cones.

After paying, we stood with them in hand and enjoyed a moment of calm before stepping back out onto the sand. I glanced at the swirl of clouds out over the ocean and said, "Weather will turn, soon."

Sam looked from the sky to me. "You Sullivans and your weather predictions. Let's enjoy another hour or two and then pack up. Do you think we have that long, oh oracle?"

I squinted at the cloud formations. Dad was much better at this than me, after his years in the navy watching storms descend on their vessel. "Yes. I can also safely predict that Theo will try to fall asleep on the ferry back after all the running around he has done today."

As I paused at the edge of the deep verandah and savoured the light breeze and coolness of the shade, I spotted a familiar swirl of chiffon. The gorgeous tangerine patterned fabric had been an impulse buy, but I was grateful that my client exclaimed in joy at seeing it. The light robe lifted with the faint wind and blew out and around Mrs Taylor.

"What on earth are you sighing over?" Sam peered out over the crowd.

I gestured with an ice cream. "Doesn't the robe look divine? There's a world of difference between a garment lifeless on a dress form to seeing it on its owner and moving in its intended environment."

"The orange and white thing? I suppose it's pretty." Sam turned a critical eye to my creation.

"Tangerine and clotted cream," I stressed the obvious difference. Mrs Taylor was a larger, older woman and the soft drapes of the chiffon and cut of the robe complimented her shape and transformed her into a regal figure.

As luck would have it, she was heading into the Pavilion and towards the changing rooms. A young woman trailed behind her, carrying a bag. Her maid, most likely. Although the disparity in their positions tugged at my heart and reminded me of a showgirl who held a secret over another young woman to force her to act as maid and secretary.

In a bold move, I veered on a course to intersect my client and managed a surprised look when we both arrived at the same point and at the same time. "Mrs Taylor, how lovely to see you."

"Hello, Mrs Devine." She stopped but had a distracted air about her.

"I do hope you are satisfied with your summer robe. It looks so lovely on you." Although I did wish she had consulted me about her hat. The arrangement was a little too heavy for the floaty robe and the orange tones were not quite right.

She attracted quite a few admiring looks with the bold choice of pattern and colour. Under the robe, Mrs Taylor wore the full swimming ensemble of pants, over-dress, stockings, and soft leather swim shoes. She had a tide line about mid-calf to show she had ventured into the ocean for a paddle.

Her fingers plucked at the rolled hem down one side. "Oh, yes. My friends are very envious, and I suspect you will have many such orders for next summer."

I murmured my thanks and made a mental note to order more chiffon in summery prints.

She peered over my shoulder and waved to someone obscured by shadows. "Now, if you'll excuse me. I must change for lunch. My son is waiting for me inside. We drove over in his new motor and it was quite the exhilarating trip, but I need a fortifying drink for the return journey."

"Of course. I hope you have a lovely afternoon and a safe drive." I stepped out of the way to allow them to pass.

"Come along, Mallory." Mrs Taylor swept away, the robe flaring out like a vibrant cloud.

The maid shot me an odd look and hurried behind, clutching the bag.

Theo's small face lit up when he saw the ice creams. As requested, I handed him one with strawberry swirls in the vanilla. We sat on the blanket watching the waves as we ate them. True to Dad's earlier prediction, the incoming tide made many people lug their belongings higher up the beach. They crowded close together in the available space on the grass, while we occupied the perfect position.

"Do you think the weather will hold another hour

or two?" I asked Dad, as I licked my chocolate ice cream cone.

He squinted and hummed as he considered the size, colour, and nature of the clouds. Then he sucked one finger and held it up to judge the light breeze. "Two I reckon. Then the wind will howl through here and clouds will dampen the sun."

With my knees drawn up to my chest and my arms around them, I smirked at Sam from over my upper arm.

She snorted and rolled her eyes.

"I had better have my swim before it gets too cold, then." Mrs Kostas threw off her towel and strode towards the water with purpose. From an older generation, she was covered from head to toe with her woollen costume, thick stockings, light shoes and a swim cap.

"It's a wonder she doesn't drown with all that clothing weighing her down," Sam muttered. "Imagine if we could swim naked instead. How freeing that would feel as the water slicked over your skin."

"Swim naked?" I stared at Sam. There were days when her comments scandalised my rule-abiding heart. Then a wicked idea popped into my head. If there was a lighter and more flexible fabric, what sort of swim costume could I construct for an active woman? My hand itched for my sketch pad. Without it, I lay back and drew scanty costumes in my mind.

Theo ran off to play with his friends. Two mothers watched the boys as they constructed elaborate sandcastles nearby. Although my son was digging trenches with lookout turrets, as he plotted an attack on the castle. With him occupied, Sam and I walked up and down the beach. We sloshed through the edge of the tide, where there was enough water to keep our feet cool, but not so far out that the water pulled against our legs.

Men were splashes of bright colour in the dark blue water. Women wore muted hues and blended with the ocean. We paused to watch a large group of young people having fun. A wave pushed their bodies towards shore. Men cheered in enjoyment as the ocean lifted their bodies and propelled them towards the sand, while the women squealed. Then they clasped hands and walked from the surf, laughing and chatting. One of their group lay on the beach, staring at the sky as though having a snooze.

Then a wave washed completely over the still form before receding.

That was odd. Why wasn't the man coughing and spluttering from the surge of sea over his face? It must have gone into his nostrils. I pulled Sam closer as one of the group bent down and shook the man by the shoulder.

"He's not breathing!" he called out to his companions.

A crowd gathered. A woman screamed. Honestly, what on earth was she screaming for? It wasn't as though someone had yelled *shark!*

The man who made the discovery pounded on the

chest of the supine gentleman who wore a red and white striped swimsuit.

Worry crawled up my chest. I wanted to give Theo a stern lecture about what happened when you ventured too far out into the ocean and got caught by the tide. I shaded my eyes as I glanced up the beach, to reassure myself that my son still played with his bucket and spade.

"That's Ricky!" Sam surged forward on recognising her employee.

I pushed to the edge of the assembled people, as Sam broke free to stand at the side of the man who made bread with her in the quiet of the morning. A half circle formed, leaving space and air for those trying to save the man. Harry appeared at my shoulder, nervous energy radiating from him.

"Ricky?" Sam called out. She crouched on the other side, as attempts to save the young man's life continued.

"It's my fault," Harry muttered.

"Of course it isn't!" Or at least it wasn't unless he held the other man's head under the water. Or played the sort of horrible prank Joseph used to do when we were children, and he would swim up under me and tug on my ankles.

I took Harry's hand. Tremors ran over his skin and up his arm. Yet the day was warm, so his shivering couldn't be from the cold. I sucked in a breath as the unexpected memory hit me with the force of a rogue wave.

Ricky laughed. 'I have a much better prospect than a poorly paid librarian. Why guzzle beer when you can sip champagne?'

Anger surged up my throat. 'If I can't have you, I'll make sure no one can!'

"Did you argue?" I blurted out.

His fingers tightened on my hand. "Yes. Apparently, a lowly librarian is not good enough for him. He told me to bugger off and leave him to have a quiet swim. If we hadn't argued, I would have been out there with him and would have seen him get into trouble."

I rubbed his arm. "I'm sure any moment now he will start coughing and throw up all that salt water in his lungs. You'll see."

The would-be-rescuer sat back on his heels, his hands on his thighs, and shook his head at an unheard question from Sam. Then he called out in a clear voice, "Someone fetch a stretcher!"

Someone else came forward and draped a towel over Ricky's head and shoulders, covering his staring eyes. As his features disappeared under the towelling, I thought about how he looked surprised. As though he hadn't expected the large wave that had knocked him off his feet. Or it might have been a rip that tangled his legs and pulled him under.

Two men trotted down from the Pavilion. Each clutched the poles of a stretcher, the brown canvas dangling between them. They placed it on the damp sand next to Ricky. Then one took hold of his shoulders, the other his feet. As they lifted him, Ricky's body rolled to his side.

On the back, a red stripe on his costume ran in a vertical line and across the others. What an odd design. Whoever made it must have mixed up their fabric patterns. Horizontal stripes on the front, and crosses on the back. But there was something about the red downward line that seemed out of place with its across neighbours. The colour and thickness were not fitting in. The line was not as sharp or straight. As the men reposition his body on the stretcher, the line gaped. There was a slice of a mere two or three inches in the wool.

Sam noticed from her position and leaned forward. Her fingers found the edge of the fabric and pulled it aside... to reveal a small vertical red line on Ricky's back. Glancing up, her gaze locked with mine and she mouthed a one worded question...

Stabbed?

Chapter Three

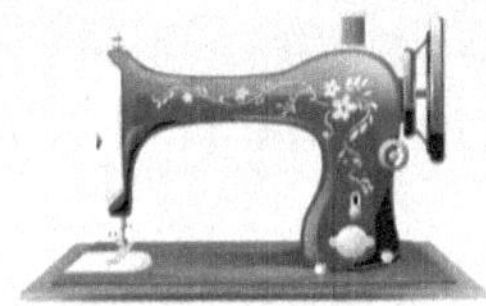

THE CROWD HAD GROWN LARGER as the men worked to save Ricky's life. Everyone on the beach knew something horrible had happened, and silence dropped as the towel-draped body was carried up the sand.

I wrapped my arm around Sam's waist.

"I have to tell Mum," she stuttered, her breath catching on a sob.

Turning, I scanned the faces to find Harry, but he had slipped away. Perhaps needing time to be alone with his grief and guilt. Dad and Mrs Kostas stood as we returned to them. Realisation was on Dad's face, and Mrs Kostas' crinkled with worry.

"It was Ricky. He drowned." Sam dropped to the blanket and grabbed a leftover scone. She picked the fluffy morsel apart but instead of eating it, she tossed fragments to an opportunistic seagull.

"Oh, no! He was such a lovely young man. With that big contagious smile and always a kind word for customers." Tears misted Mrs Kostas' eyes, and she pulled a handkerchief from her pocket to dab at them.

"Poor bugger." Dad dropped back into his deckchair. "Must have gone out too deep or got caught in a rip."

"There was an odd tear in his swimsuit." I kept seeing the small gap in the fabric and the wound on Ricky's back.

"That happens. Lots of bits of wood and things bobbing around out there that a body can bash up against. You'd be surprised what we used to find even out in the deep ocean." Dad picked up a thermos and poured out the last of the tea.

I fetched Theo, as mothers gathered up their offspring, needing the comfort of having them within arm's reach.

"Did a man die?" he asked with wide-eyed innocence.

"Yes. He must have got into trouble out in the water. That's why your swimming lessons are so important." I propelled him back to our blanket, and he dropped beside his grandfather.

Dad ruffled Theo's hair, his hat dangling down his back and the string tight against his neck. "In the olden days, many sailors couldn't swim. They thought if you learned how, it meant you didn't trust the captain."

Theo screwed up his face. "That sounds silly."

Dad nodded. "It was, but we know better nowadays. It's very important that sailors, or anyone living by the water, know how to swim."

A dead body washing ashore put a dampener on the afternoon, and people packed up to leave. Someone had telephoned the authorities, and as we prepared to leave an hour later, two motor vehicles pulled into the gravelled area beside the Pavilion. One had the long body and ominous dark shape of the vehicle used to transport bodies to the morgue. From the other motorcar stepped three men. Two in the distinctive uniform of policemen.

The other figure among them drew my attention.

Detective Archer.

Even in the summer warmth, he wore a dark grey three-piece suit. His fedora sat at a jaunty angle, or it might have knocked against the interior of the vehicle. He scanned the crowd as people flowed towards the wharf. Somehow, his gaze settled on me and singled me out. His body stilled for a moment. Then he touched the brim of his hat in recognition before the constable at his side pulled his attention away.

A tingle shot through my body and out of my toes. After our previous tangle, I had a subconscious guilty feeling. Not that I had anything to do with Ricky's death. It was a horrible accident. The sort that sadly happened all too often, when we flocked to the beaches over summer.

Trying to cast off the desire to confess, I concentrated on packing everything up and returning the deckchairs and umbrella. Then we joined the queue waiting for the next sailing. Getting back on the ferry took much longer than the trip out. Two hot and bothered policemen were writing down everyone's name before we were allowed on the vessel. People around me grumbled at the delay as we stood under the sun. The heat was tempered by the clouds that Dad had predicted would roll in.

"This is bloody stupid. The chap drowned. Why should we be inconvenienced?" the man behind me complained.

My mind couldn't stop unseeing the moment when Sam placed a finger in the slice and tugged at the fabric, revealing a corresponding wound in Ricky's back. But he had to have drowned, surely? As Dad said, the gash was most likely caused by colliding with something on his journey back to shore. Either a piece of wood or rubbish tossed by some careless individual into the water. It wasn't as though sharp, pointy metal things like knives could float, stab someone, and then sink to the ocean floor.

So why did the injury bother me so much? Most likely my recent encounter with the law and being labelled as a murder suspect made me skittish to be around any sudden death or accident. The way the detective had stilled and pinned me where I stood made an unreasonable and silly fear surge up my throat. Would I be blamed for this death?

Soon our turn came to step onto the steamer, and we gave the names of our group and address in Ascot Street. Then we were waved through by the constable. With relief, I sank to the bench at the bow. A chill rippled over my flesh, and I rubbed it away as I lectured myself that Ricky's death was an accident and nothing more. Except the memory that worried him as he exited the toilet wouldn't stop replaying behind my eyes.

You know what we do to traitors.

An idea popped into my head. What if he had spied for the Germans during the war, and someone had found out? Gosh. I thought supporting Australia in rugby was bad enough. If Ricky had been a double agent, that would certainly have preyed on his mind during peacetime. Especially if he encountered someone who knew his secret, and he feared exposure.

Theo knelt on the bench and leaned over the side. Dad stomped his foot against the wooden boards from beside me.

"How's the foot?" I asked as he angled his body to have a hand free to grab Theo if the lad leaned too far out.

He slapped his knee. "Better for a good salty drink. It's bloody daft that a missing foot should itch like it does."

"Perhaps your brain doesn't know it's gone." Just as Dad worried about me, I worried about him. Which of us had more cause for concern?

"That would explain the number of times I fall over getting up to go to the loo in the night. My brain is sure I have two feet." He huffed a quiet chuckle.

I leaned against Dad's shoulder. He definitely gave me more to worry about. While I had made the odd foolish decision in my life, I hadn't played soccer with a live round and blown my foot off.

The excitement of the day and too much sunshine took their toll on little Theo. True to my prediction, he tried to doze on the return trip, but the steamer ploughing into waves kept jerking him awake. Just as Dad had said, the wind arrived and whipped the harbour into small peaks. Clouds scuttled across the sun and people in thin, damp clothes shivered as chills swept over them.

Once off the boat, we found a horse-drawn cart for hire and loaded ourselves and the baskets onto the back. Sam and I sat at the back edge, dangling our feet off the side for the short journey up to Thorndon. Dad paid the man while we unloaded everything. Then the driver turned his horse and cart around to trot back to the wharf.

"He'll sleep well tonight." Dad gestured to Theo, the child's eyelids heavy.

"An early bath, dinner, and bed, I think." Then my concerns turned from the sleepy child to Sam. "Will you and your mum be all right?"

Sam nodded, but there was an air of heavy sadness about the Kostases. "I still can't believe Ricky is gone. He hadn't worked in the bakery with us for long. Not quite a year, but he was a cheerful chap, and I'll miss his chatter in the mornings."

I squeezed her hands. "You know where I am if you want to talk. Or not talk."

She nodded, on the verge of walking away, when she turned back with a crinkle to her brow. "Do you have any plans to see Frank tomorrow?"

What an odd question. "No. Why?"

"It's a leap year. If he wants to see you tomorrow, he might expect a proposal. So promise you will avoid him if he comes calling," she warned me.

I'd forgotten that tomorrow was the twenty-ninth of February. I might be a modern woman who juggled family and working, but I wasn't so forward as to propose to Frank...or *any* man, for that matter. A snort burst from me at the idea of getting on bended knee before the lanky Frank. "An easy promise to make."

Reassured, she let go of my hand and slipped into her cottage as a misty rain began to fall.

Having avoided single men who secretly desired a leap-day marriage proposal on Sunday, Monday morning I sat at the table chewing toast as I scanned the newspaper. At least there was no front-page headline screaming *wartime spy executed on beach!* I took that as a good sign. On page three was a tiny article about the tragic death at Days Bay and then a few pivotal words... *police are currently investigating circumstances surrounding the death.*

I dropped Theo at the childminder with minimal grumbles. Then I walked down to my shop. Etty and I had a busy day, and it seemed each week saw more new customers coming through the door. The odd bang came from upstairs through the morning, as Dad worked to transform the first floor into a workroom and luxurious fitting rooms.

After a long day, I headed home. Theo was busy at the kitchen table with a colouring book. His coloured pencils were kept in a wooden box Dad had made for him. I smoothed a lock of Theo's hair and planted a kiss on his head. A delicious aroma came from the stove, and I cracked it open to see the casserole dish inside.

Dad sat in his armchair and put his book aside. "Busy day, love?"

"Yes." I lowered myself to the other chair and toed off my shoes. "But I'll not complain about customers happy to pay a deposit before I even open my sketch pad."

Our lives might have been ordinary and working class, but from the comfort of our cottage at the bottom of the globe, a girl could dream of exotic locations and the gowns women would wear to dance to the new jazz music. As Dad read, I sketched fanciful designs for no client in particular. My imagination was free to swoop with the pencil and craft fairytale dresses that made my soul soar.

That night, and feeling somewhat ghoulish, I found the newspaper and turned to the obituaries' sections. Running my finger down the list of names, I stopped at the small entry for *Hammond, Richard*. A weight pressed on my heart to see a young, vibrant life reduced to a few short lines in a narrow column of the newspaper.

Beloved son and loyal soldier. Survived by his mother and grandfather.

"Ricky's funeral notice is in the paper. It's on Thursday," I said to Dad. "It sounds like his mother is still alive, but not his father." Once more I would ask Etty to take care of the shop while we farewelled someone taken far too early.

My heart tightened to imagine his mother's pain. To bury a son seemed unimaginable. Especially when she must have breathed a sigh of relief to have him home safe and sound from war. I glanced at Theo, my maternal instinct needing reassurance that he still lived and breathed. As evidenced by his ability to smear marmite around his mouth and fingers, completely unaware of the mess he made.

"Poor bugger. But life's not fair, and many a good man and woman have gone into the ground over the last six years." Dad snapped the sports section open and disappeared behind the pages.

Sometimes, I wondered if Dad felt he missed out on the action when our lads mobilised and headed off to Europe. He never said if he did. But I heard it sometimes, in the tone of his voice. An edge, as if he wondered what might have been. Personally, I was glad his status as a medically discharged sailor with only one foot to stand on, kept him on our shores. Our family was far too small to be carved any smaller by a mortar or pandemic.

I tucked my grief and heaviness of heart inside me

and smiled at my son. "Make sure you wash your face and hands before dinner. Don't just lick the crayon off."

Thursday morning, I donned my black dress and tugged my short gloves on my hands. I met Sam and her mother outside, and we walked down to the end of Lambton Quay to catch a tram to the funeral. We were each lost in our own thoughts for the short ride along the quay and up Willis Street to the church. As we hopped off the tram, I glanced upward and thought the Presbyterian church was rather smart with its cream exterior and bright red roof tiles. Or was it more orange?

Sam tugged me inside as I wanted to linger and contemplate the exact shade.

The church had served Wellington since the very beginning of the city. The first settlers back in 1840 had built a wooden church on the site. Over the years, it continued to serve the community, and the grand church we entered was the most recent incarnation.

Inside, there didn't seem to be a fraction of the crowd that the death of popular showgirl Agatha Marshall had attracted. But then her service had been in a much smaller church. St John's could seat over 800 and the friends and family of Ricky were scattered among the pews like beads on tulle. Scanning the crowd, I looked for any familiar faces. A pale and drawn one caught my eye. Harry moved from his spot pressed to the back wall and joined us. As though he waited for someone he knew before venturing down the aisle.

Together, we picked a row in the middle and took our seats. Ricky's mother and grandfather sat at the front but didn't speak. The readings were made by chaps who had served alongside Ricky. They all spoke of his cheerful disposition and easy-going attitude. The hymns were a celebration of his life but tinged with the deep sadness of him never reaching his full potential.

We all stood as the family accompanied the coffin on its last journey. As it passed by, we filed in behind on our way out. Near the back, a large woman sitting alone lifted her veil to dab at her eyes. My feet froze to the ground and Sam nearly stumbled at my sudden halt. I recognised the face in an instant, even when she hurriedly dropped the thick veil back into place after noisily blowing her nose.

Mrs Taylor. My older but still fashionable client, whom I had seen at the Pavilion the day Ricky died.

Chapter Four

Sam apologised to the people behind me who were blocked by my still form and tugged me back into motion and towards the door.

Once outside we stepped to one side, and I whispered, "That was Mrs Taylor. My client. How does she know Ricky?"

Sam shrugged as we watched the coffin loaded into the hearse for the trip to the cemetery in Karori. "Kostas Bakery is very popular. Maybe Ricky used to serve her when she bought a sausage roll."

I only glimpsed her for a few seconds, but her eyes were red from crying. No one got that upset over a sausage roll. Not even Theo when he once lost his grip on a warm one, and it tumbled to the ground.

"A friend of the family, perhaps?" Mrs Kostas said from my side.

That seemed far more likely. Mrs Taylor would be of a similar age to Mrs Hammond, and they might have moved in the same circles. "You're probably right, Mrs Kostas. She might fondly remember Ricky as a young lad."

The wind picked up and forced us to hurry along. Harry tugged his hat low, waved an unsteady goodbye, and then jumped onto a tram heading in the direction of the university.

Mrs Kostas clutched her handbag and marched with a determined step. We trailed behind her.

"Harry's taking it hard," I murmured to Sam.

"Worry gnaws at him. He thinks that if they hadn't argued, he would have been swimming alongside Ricky and could have saved him." Sam had my hand tucked into her crooked arm and we leaned our heads together to talk in a low tone.

Being unable to save a friend would weigh someone down. So would striking out in anger. But I held my silence. Now wasn't the time to pick over how exactly Ricky had met his end. Silently, I hoped Dad was right and a stray bit of wood or something had torn the red-striped swimming costume.

We veered onto Boulcott Street, the Kostases heading towards their bakery on the Terrace. I squeezed Sam's hand and took Plimmer Steps down to my workshop. I found Etty in an odd mood. My usually cheerful assistant muttering under her breath and in a rare display of exasperation she tossed a piece to her worktable.

"I'm sorry, Etty, to leave you to work alone this morning while I went to the funeral. I shall make it up to you by letting you have a half-day off on Friday. You can leave at lunchtime as a thank you." Since her foul mood seemed to be due to my absence, I offered an apology and an olive branch. There were only two of us in the small space, and I didn't like having half the workforce angry at me.

"Oh, Mrs Devine! It's not you. It's my stupid brother and his stupid friends." She rose from her chair and approached where I sat.

"Well, I am relieved you are not upset at me. But what has your brother done that has set you to fuming all morning long?" I didn't have a brother so had no experience with annoying siblings, only gangly and gullible cousins. I set aside the hand sewing to give her my full attention.

Her fair brow pulled into a frown. "Patrick is always getting himself in trouble. Came home last night with bruises on his knuckles, and we know he's been fighting. Da would have taken the strap to him if he hadn't grown so tall."

I suspected every mother worried about her son falling in with the wrong crowd, and I would have to navigate those waters in the coming years. "Do you think it's his friends?"

She huffed. "Yes. He's fallen under the spell of some old rugby player called Geoff who was injured at Gallipoli. Thinks the sun rises and sets from his...well, I think you know where. Patrick was too young to sign up, and he idolises soldiers with their war stories. I think he's daft. War was horrid," her voice fell to a whisper.

"I suspect only those who have never seen battle and the horrors of the trenches think there is anything to idolise about it. Our lads thought it would be a grand adventure when they shipped out. None of us knew what they would endure to survive." Or not. I rubbed the gold band on my finger. Freddie Devine never returned and was buried on a battlefield far away.

"Anyway, Patrick got into a huge row with Ma and Da last night when he finally crawled home. Da says they came here to live to keep us away from the troubles in Ireland. But I worry Patrick is heading down the wrong path and don't know what to do." Tears shimmered in Etty's hazel eyes.

"It sounds like you need to find a way to get your brother away from the influence of this Geoff and around friends who don't get into so many fights." My brain spun. If I remembered correctly her younger brother had recently turned eighteen.

"I wish it was that easy. He works on the docks, and I suspect many of them have Irish blood in their veins the way they can sniff out a brawl." Etty leaned on the cutting table and tapped her fingers against the side.

"If we put our heads together, I'm sure we could think of a way to direct him towards a new crowd. What of his other interests? I know my cousin spends most of his evenings tending to his motorcycle." Perhaps what Patrick needed was a time-consuming hobby that left little time for wandering the streets, looking for trouble.

"Do you mean Constable Sullivan?" Etty's voice stumbled over Joseph's name.

"Yes. Joseph. Do you think Patrick would like to learn about motorcycles? If he was keen, I could ask Joseph if he would help?" My interest rose even further as a gentle blush of colour washed over Etty's face.

"Oh, yes. That would be grand, Mrs Devine. Patrick is ever so good with mechanical things." Her words came out in a breathy rush. Then a frown worried at her forehead again. "But he's got a horrid attitude towards the police."

"Well, why don't you see if you can talk Patrick around to the idea, and then I will ask Joseph?" At which point I shall insist that Etty accompany her brother when I introduce him to Joseph. The beginnings of a plan spun in the back of my head. One that, I hoped, might bring some joy back into my cousin's life.

Having cleared the topic that was causing Etty concern, we fell back into the rhythm of our day. Before we knew it, the clock chimed four. Another day was crossed off the calendar, and we were another day closer to completing the new space upstairs.

"We need to decide on wallpaper so I can hang it in the fitting rooms," I said to Etty as we hung up our aprons and tidied away our projects.

"It's ever so exciting. You're going to need more hands too, to sew all the new commissions we will have. Especially after the dance for the prince. What a chance to dazzle society with your creations!" Etty's hazel eyes gleamed as she glanced at the ceiling, no doubt imagining what we would create in the light-filled atelier.

The grand evening in honour of the Prince of Wales's visit was still two months away, and I wondered if we would have everything finished in time. "And a shop girl or two, for when we turn this space into a shop for the ready-to-wear collection."

My assistant's excitement was infectious. My mind bounded ahead to all the glorious fabrics we would have upstairs, and dress forms with stunning outfits. I preferred to skirt around the business side of hiring and training new employees. Let alone the worry of if we would bring enough in to pay for everything.

That evening after dinner, Dad and I sat listening to the wireless while Theo played with toy cars on the rug. I had a piece of cotton on my lap and worked with a bright pink silk thread to make lines of smocking through the pinned pleats. Once done, it would make a lovely dress for a little girl. Not something I usually did, but I thought offering matching outfits for mothers and daughters would look smart in the new shop.

The news reporter read a snippet in the bulletin that caught my attention and my hand stilled.

"Last weekend's death at Days Bay of Mr Richard Hammond has been deemed non-accidental, and the police are investigating," said the crisp British accent coming from the wireless.

That made my eyebrows shoot up.

Dad huffed. "Well, that's daft. Normally when you pull them out of the water, they've drowned. Unless your ship was torpedoed. Some of those poor lads never had the chance to drown."

Harry's memory flared over my skin once more, with the hastily flung words in the heat of an argument. I shook it off. A librarian couldn't commit such a crime of passion. Surely it wasn't in their nature?

That day rushed back to me, as Sam's finger found the slice in the fabric as Ricky's body was rolled to go on the stretcher. "There was a tear in the back of his swimsuit and a matching wound in his skin. Other than that, I can't recollect seeing any injuries about him." Although I was trained to stitch satin, not flesh, and had never been to medical school. I'm sure Etty would regale me with innumerable ways one could die naturally while swimming. Like some form of stroke—other than breaststroke. But if the police ruled it non-accidental, that meant their examining physician had decided it was no heart attack or something similar.

"I'm sure that detective will figure it out." Dad's attention dropped back to his book.

Mention of *that detective* conjured the image to my mind of Detective Archer, standing motionless as policemen climbed from their vehicle at Days Bay. His dark gaze fixing me on the sand.

What had flashed through his mind in that moment of recognition? Perhaps he recalled some file on me at police headquarters that labelled me as an argumentative troublemaker with the capacity to kill.

"I'm going to check on Sam and her mum. See how they are getting on." I placed my sewing back in the basket and dashed from the back door of our cottage to that of the Kostas women. Pausing briefly, I rapped on the glass before I barged in.

Sam stood alone in the kitchen, heating milk in a pan. She regarded me with sad eyes.

I hugged my friend tight. "How was the rest of your day?"

She tested the temperature of the milk with a fingertip. Satisfied, she spooned in the cocoa powder. "I think it was worse than Saturday and seeing him wash up. The bakery's so quiet without him. Mum's gone to bed, and I said I'd take her through a cocoa."

After Sam saw to her mum, we curled up in her lounge. Sam at one end of the long sofa, one leg tucked up under her. In her hands, she held a large mug of cocoa. "That detective came to see us at the bakery this afternoon. He asked all sorts of questions about Ricky and wanted to know of any disputes we had with him or ones we overheard. Joseph was with him and whispered that Ricky hadn't drowned, as there was no water in his lungs."

"We just heard the news on the radio." The air left my lungs with a whoosh. Even though we had heard that Ricky hadn't drowned over the wireless, it still took me by surprise that one person could snuff out the life of another. I understood our boys fighting for their lives and our freedom, but during peacetime, it shouldn't happen. "Are they sure?"

Sam nodded. "Stabbed in the back. The knife punctured his heart, poor bugger."

My mind splintered in two directions. One part was miffed that Joseph confided in Sam about how Ricky had died, when I practically had to corner him in a shed to find out details about the investigation into Agatha's death. The other part of me wanted to know how such a crime was committed while out swimming. The latter part won. "How does that even happen? Who conceals a knife in their swimsuit to stab an unsuspecting bather?" A mad slasher in the shallows would have caused mass panic, but nothing interrupted the enjoyment of a lazy summer day until Ricky washed ashore.

Sam stared at me over the rim of her mug. "I've given that some thought..."

There was a thought that gave me pause. Did my friend often spend time contemplating how to kill people?

"And I reckon he was killed somewhere else and tossed in the water. Then the incoming tide washed him back towards shore."

"Where would it have happened, though?" The bay had a gentle curve. It wasn't like rocky outcrops broke it up. That was why we all flocked there on a nice day—for the wide expanse of golden sand. As much as I loved living in Wellington, we were deprived of beaches and the curve of the harbour was nothing but rocky outcrops. The ocean butted up against the feet of the city. There was a handkerchief of beach at Oriental

Bay, but on a nice day, it was comparable to being a sardine in a tin, as civilised folk fought over a spot.

Sam shrugged. "The wharf, most likely. Or he could have had an argument with someone farther around, where there were fewer people."

My concern was less for poor Ricky, who was now beyond such mortal concerns, than my friend. "How are you coping?"

She flashed me a smile, and it quickly dropped away. "I miss him. He was a chatty bugger. Used to drive me nuts some mornings when I wanted to work in silence. Funny how now the bakery seems too quiet without him."

"I imagine your customers will miss him, too."

Four mornings a week, Ricky rose early to help Sam, then he served in the shop until noon. Young, handsome, and with a friendly disposition, he could chat up anyone who walked in and persuade them to buy whatever was on special.

Sam sipped her cocoa. It was a few quiet minutes before she continued talking. "People are coming in just to say how sorry they are and that they will miss his smiling face. Mum and I are run off our feet. Vita is filling in with the early shift, but her husband is grumbling about being left with the kids, and she won't be able to do it for long."

"What about Harry? How close were he and Ricky?" The two men had engaged in an odd dance, circling each other without wanting anyone else to know there was a possibility of being more than *chums*.

After he slipped away at the beach, I hadn't seen him on the return ferry.

Sam's lips pulled in a wry expression. "Not as close as he wanted to be, but close enough that he's taking it hard."

Chapter Five

FRIDAY and the weekend had passed uneventfully. I immersed myself in wallpaper samples trying to decide on the perfect pattern for the new fitting rooms. Finally, after consulting with Mrs Cooper, we settled on a pale grey and white geometric pattern with a silver line. It was subtle, but terribly modern at the same time.

Monday afternoon, the bell rang in my workshop and an unexpected sight stood in my doorway, Sam and Harry. The latter with wide eyes and a pale complexion that looked sickly, rather than delicate. His eyes were red-rimmed, and he seemed to be on the verge of bursting into tears.

"Do you have a moment for a quiet chat?" Sam smiled at Etty.

I stared around me. We had four dress forms, all in various stages of being pinned and clothed. A stack of pattern pieces sat on the cutting table, waiting for me to finish spreading a length of fabric. More clothing waited in baskets by the Singer for machine stitching. Another piece draped over the arm of my chair needed hand work. I might have a mere second to spare, but no longer. But Sam wouldn't have asked if it wasn't important and given the state of Harry, a chill gave me an idea what it might be about.

With a sigh, I gestured upstairs. "Let's pop upstairs to talk." Something about the tense set of her jaw suggested Sam wanted privacy, even from my loyal assistant. "I won't be long, Etty."

We dashed out my door and along a few strides to the little foyer for upstairs. We took the steep steps in silence. I always kept one hand on the balustrade since my near-fatal fall down them. Dad had been busy and soon we could start decorating the former bedrooms that would now become luxurious fitting rooms. He had even installed a sinuously curved desk where, one day, a receptionist could sit. At the rear would be a large workroom, my office, storage, and even a small room for staff to eat lunch and brew a cup of tea. What bliss!

Although the idea of finding and hiring staff almost made me break out in hives. Luckily, I had Sam and Mrs Cooper to advise me about managing others. The idea formed in my head of promoting Etty, as my loyal second in command. But I was rushing ahead of myself.

"What is it? Nothing good I am guessing by the state of Harry." My attention darted to the slender man. Given the flustered state of him, I could take a good stab in the dark at the problem. Or stab on a beach.

"Detective Archer interviewed me this morning about Ricky. Apparently, we were seen arguing at Days Bay that Saturday." He licked his lips and paced across the floor as he spoke.

"Sounds familiar." My tangle with the law had started in a similar fashion. Pedestrians in Plimmer Steps had reported my disagreement with a client. The difference here was I had known I was innocent. Could I say the same about Sam's friend? Experience taught me that murderous minds could lurk behind the quietest exteriors.

"We need to find out who killed Ricky," Sam spoke with a clear and strong tone.

"I'm a seamstress, not a sleuth." An apologetic smile crossed my lips. While I was sympathetic to Harry's predicament, I wasn't sure I could help. Or even if I wanted to assist. My plate was full with commissions, and who knew when I could find time to poke into Ricky's death?

"Come on, Grace. We did pretty well as a team to uncover that Lynn Young murdered Agatha Marshall. I think we have a shot to find the truth here, too. Besides, there are things about Ricky that *we* know, that I am betting the police don't know. Nor do we want *that* truth to be widely circulated." Sam crossed her arms.

I read between the lines. Antiquated laws took a

dim view of the private activities of citizens of the same gender. Personally, I thought it was nobody's business except those involved. Sadly, there were some individuals in society who waged personal wars against anybody they deemed *different* from them. That description included men like Harry and Ricky and women like Sam and her friend Estelle.

Even if proven innocent, Harry could lose his job at the university if they reported his romantic preferences in the newspaper. A law school doesn't like that sort of scandal attached to its staff. Why were some so afraid of anybody who wasn't a cookie-cutter image of themselves? Differences made life more vibrant and interesting. I shuddered at the impact on fashion if we were only ever allowed to use one type of cloth, in one particular pattern and colour. It would be akin to prison uniforms.

Sam arched one eyebrow. She knew exactly how to draw me into the intrigue—by ruffling my sense of equality and fairness.

"Do you think that was why someone killed Ricky... because of his private life?" Sadly if that were the case, Ricky wasn't the first man to die because of how he was made. Nor would he be the last until something changed in society.

Be the change you want to see, Dad would say. Or some similarly sage response would have come from his aged and linseed oil soaked brain.

"Possibly." Harry took out a handkerchief and blew

his nose. "In the last year, at least five lads have been ambushed in dark alleys and beaten. It's made us all nervous. Like cats running across a hot tin roof."

Outrage flared inside me. "Beaten? That's... monstrous. Why has it not been in the papers? Why aren't the police..."

The quiet looks on their faces silenced the words flowing over my tongue. Of course the papers weren't going to report, let alone condemn, attacks on those who preferred the company of the same sex. That was the exact same reason why the police weren't looking into it. Assuming they even knew about the assaults.

My shoulders heaved. "Did the men report the assaults to the police?"

Harry's lips thinned.

No. Of course they told no one. Except to warn others like them. What was wrong with people? While slow to anger, my blood heated as Harry alluded to the torments of trying to live a life true to who he was.

"Very well. If you want me to help, then you need to tell us what happened that day. And it has to be the complete truth. No leaving anything out." There was a chair leaning against the wall, probably where Dad sat while having his break. I pushed it towards Harry and indicated for him to sit.

He stared at the chair. "I can't sit while you two stand. That's not right."

In detective novels, the suspect always sat while the detectives loomed over him. Besides, I didn't want

Harry wandering around as he told his version of events. I wanted to watch him. He might have tells when he was fibbing. Like Theo, who couldn't leave the bottom button of his shirt alone while he tried to claim no knowledge of where the last biscuit in the tin had gone. "This isn't the time to be gentlemanly. Sit and start talking."

He dropped to the seat and heaved a sigh, then began. "Friday I saw Ricky at the bakery. I said how the weather was supposed to be a cracker that weekend and summer was nearly over. I asked if he wanted to go to the bay with me and a few lads on Saturday." He squirmed, as though the seat wasn't big enough for his bottom.

"Were there any other lads going?" I already knew the answer but wanted to test his honesty.

He cast his eyes downward. "No. I figured he wouldn't go if he knew it was just the two of us. On a date."

Sam cuffed her friend on the back of the head, and he let out a muffled yelp. "You idiot. You don't lie to someone to get them to go out with you, then act surprised when he catches you out and gets angry. Not to mention you put him in a horribly awkward situation."

Since Sam was dishing out the reprimands, that made her the bad cop. I'd be the good one, a role that came more naturally to me anyway. "It's not easy, is it? When you like someone, but you're not sure if they like you. I imagine it's even harder when you can't be open about your feelings. The prejudices of others make you vulnerable."

He flashed me a sad smile. "It's an odd dance we are forced to do. Finding ways to pose a question without saying the words out loud. I thought if he spent more time with me, I could figure out if he was, you know, *interested* or not. We always had a laugh and a good time whenever we met up at the clubs and it felt...*real* this time."

"When did he realise he wasn't part of a larger group?" Sam got our interrogation back on track.

"Not until after the steamer had left the wharf. I told him the others must have been onboard already, and we needed to find them. I pretended to search for a bit around the decks. Until he realised I hadn't been entirely honest." Colour flushed from under Harry's collar at the admission and he tugged on the starched fabric around his neck.

"Did you argue?" I knew they had a falling out, but didn't know the surrounding circumstances.

Harry blew out a snort. "Not there, no. Too many people around and kids running back and forth. He got the huff and sat off to one side. He must have seen someone he knew though, because I saw him chatting to another chap. Burly fellow with cauliflower ears and a misshapen nose. Then Ricky rushed off somewhere."

That must have been when I encountered him outside the toilets. The memory closest to his mind had been about being told *you don't betray your team.* Harry's description confirmed my view that the memory was a conflict over rugby. Cauliflower ear was a common problem among rugby players. Scrums, tackles, and on-field collisions caused injuries to the ears which, over time, led to deformities that somewhat resembled cauliflower.

"Did you see him again on the steamer?" Now I wondered when the argument with Harry had occurred.

"No. It was later that day. Probably mid-morning. I was wandering like a lost dog trying to find him. I finally found his hiding spot under the wharf supports, on the other side of the beach where there weren't any people. He was there all alone, having a cigarette." Harry's long-fingered hands curled into fists.

"Then you had your argument, where no one could hear or see you," I whispered the words.

He nodded, his Adam's apple bobbing against his collar and tie. "I told him I wanted to know where things stood between us. I'm such a fool. I like...liked... him so much. I carved myself open and served up my heart on a platter. I thought he liked me, too, and we could make a go of it."

Carving himself open was an unfortunate metaphor in the circumstances.

"He rejected you. The bugger." Sam put her hands on her hips. Her disapproval turned on her deceased employee.

"He said I wasn't good enough for him. That he had met someone who promised him life on easy street." Unshed tears shimmered in Harry's eyes when he raised his head. But were they from the pain of heartbreak, or remorse for what he had done?

The argument played out in my head. *Why guzzle beer when you can sip champagne?* Who was the other person whom Ricky referred to? But it was Harry's words flung in anger, that played over and over in my mind. *If I can't have you, I'll make sure no one can!*

"You were rejected and angry about it." When I touched someone and their memory leapt into my head, I experienced the same feelings as them in that moment. As clear as day, I recalled the anger surging up Harry's throat as he issued his threat. Had he plunged a knife into Ricky's back in the heat of their fight?

I glanced at Sam and rolled my eyes to the side. She frowned. I tried again, sliding one hand up nonchalantly to tap the side of my head, and then I rolled my eyes again. This time, she caught my subtle clue.

"Did you do it, Harry?" Sam asked.

He gasped, and his head shot up. "No! I swear. He told me to get lost and then stormed off under the wharf. That was the last I saw of him. Until..."

Until he washed up. Dead.

Harry leapt to his feet and paced the floor. I couldn't see us getting much more out of him as his state of agitation increased. Time to move to a different topic.

"If it wasn't Harry, then who killed Ricky? Someone must have had a reason to stab him. What do we know about Ricky? Did he live with his mother or alone? What does he do outside of working at the bakery?" The young man had worked for Sam for only a year. I tried to recall all the times I had been in the store and chatted with him. Had he let slip anything that hinted about problems in his life and anyone who might hold a fatal grudge? I scratched at my memory like a chicken in the dirt, seeking to bring something to the surface.

"He worked four days a week in the bakery. When I think about it, he was always chatty but asking about other people or what was in the newspaper. I can't remember him ever really talking about *himself*," Sam said.

We both turned to Harry, hoping he could cast more light into the dim recesses of the murdered man's life. Unfortunately, he shook his head.

"I don't know anything about his family, or where he lives. He wouldn't tell me. He kept his private life clammed shut tighter than an oyster. Almost like he didn't trust me," he muttered. Leaning against the wall, he stared at his hands and tugged his cuff into alignment with his jacket sleeve.

Sam stared at me, as though I knew what to do. Honestly. Being a suspect in one murder enquiry didn't make me a detective. But I had a few ideas. "What about the bakery records? Did he put an address down when he applied for the job?"

Sam's eyes lit up. "Good idea. I'll go search my records, see what I can find, and report back to you."

"I'll keep my ears open, and see if I can rustle up anything more about Ricky's private life," Harry said.

"I have to go back to work. Harry, if you remember or find anything, anything at all, that you think might be relevant, then tell Sam or me." Leaving them to it, I trotted down the stairs (one hand tight on the rail) and headed back to my waiting commissions.

Chapter Six

Drawing a sketch of a gown was a magical process. So was seeing the finished result on a client and watching the joy on their faces as they turned before the mirror. What happened between those two stages was anything but magical, and involved sweat, tears, blood (when we stabbed our fingers) and salty curses learned at my seafaring father's knee.

A new design had no pattern, so Etty and I had to make them and usually from scratch. Rarely we might borrow a piece or two from something similar. Using muslin, we cut shapes, draped, and pinned them to a dress form until we achieved in fabric the same result as a pencil on paper. Only then did we take the material and turn them into paper pieces that could be laid out on fabric for the final garment.

Before we were interrupted by Sam and Harry, Etty and I worked on a gown for the forthcoming gala ball for the Prince of Wales. The piece would be, in my humble opinion, a showstopper. Miss Belmont would be unrivalled. Or she would be if we could get the fabric to co-operate. The gown had an echo of Edwardian fashion in the narrow skirt and asymmetrical train but with a modern 1920s twist. The front overlapped to create a cutaway to scandalously reveal calves and almost...knees. On the other side to the train, fabric draped in a sort of peplum that hung to one side. The bodice had a low back and a draped front.

Etty and I had worked most of the day, trying to translate my drawing into a working model, but the fabric refused to co-operate.

"What about if we shorten this piece and add a dart?" Etty unpinned a bit of the peplum and folded a dart between her fingers. Then she repined it at a slightly different angle.

"Yes. That looks better. But the drape still doesn't look right." I wanted the gown to look effortless. As though we had simply taken a bolt of fabric and thrown it over the client. But that required an awful lot of work and construction.

The clock chimed four, and I glanced up. I liked to close up around four, as that gave me time to tidy away the day's work before I faced the walk home. "Let's tackle this fresh tomorrow."

Etty swept the floor while I threw sheets over the forms and wheeled them deeper into the shop and away from prying eyes looking through the wide window. Then we said our goodnights.

Sam waited for me when I got home, her presence

obvious as I walked along the narrow covered path to the rear of the house. A delicious aroma wafted out the window, and I closed my eyes and inhaled for a moment. Pushing open the back door, my friend stood at the bench and showed Theo how to roll dough into balls and then squish them down, to make biscuits. My son stole pinches of dough when he thought my friend wasn't looking.

"You two look as though you have been busy." I kissed Theo's head.

"Aunty Sam says I could be a baker one day. I do like to eat biscuits." A serious frown marred Theo's young forehead as he contemplated a future surrounded by sweetened dough.

I ruffled his hair. "No need to decide just yet."

"I found Ricky's address. He lives up the way on Governor Road, just off The Rigi." Sam gestured with her head in the general direction beyond the Botanic Gardens.

The Rigi was a steep slash of road with a nearly one hundred and eighty degree corner as it carved a path to Northland, the little suburb that sat up on the hill above us.

"Do you know if he lives there with his mother?" I stole a warm biscuit from the cooling tray and winked at Theo. The scamp grinned and grabbed one for himself before hurrying away with his prize.

Sam finished pressing down the last batch of biscuits and slid them into the oven. "Don't know. The form he gave me ages ago only has an address on it."

We didn't learn much from the funeral either. There was no mention of other family or siblings. We'd have no idea of exactly who we'd find at his home until we turned up on the doorstep to ask our impertinent questions prying into his private affairs. "Could you bake a pie, please, so we don't turn up empty-handed?"

She glanced at her watch. "Of course. If you watch these and take them out in ten minutes, I'll whip up a pie now."

I shrugged off my coat and hung it beside the back door. "We could go after dinner? It's still light enough and we don't have far to go."

We made a plan to meet at seven. That gave us time to have dinner and for me to have Theo bathed and in his pyjamas for story time with his poppa.

Later that evening, I headed out the front door. Sam already waited for me with a savoury pie nestled in a sort of canvas sling for our walk. We headed up the walkway to Tinakori Road and turned left towards the Botanic Gardens. The straight stretch of road changed its name to Glenmore Street. Across from the gardens, carved through the bush, was the steep road known as The Rigi. At the treacherous corner that had seen a few vehicles tumble, we struck out along Governor Road. We kept heading upward and aimed for a small grouping of four homes, clustered among the greenery.

"Twelve, here it is." Sam gestured to a path that angled away from the road. Our destination was one of the middle four cottages.

"At least someone is home," I murmured. A light

glowed in the front window, although no one moved in front of it. What if Ricky had left it on when he departed that Saturday morning?

Once up the path, we paused and had a moment at the bottom of the step to the front door. Sam looked at me. I looked at her. Then my friend raised her dark eyebrows.

"You were Ricky's employer. You should go first." A nudge with my elbow propelled her into the front position.

Sam knocked, and a mixture of relief and anxiety flowed through me at the sounds from within. The door was flung open by a gentleman in his late twenties. His light brown hair was in disarray, as though he had been tugging on it. Dark-rimmed spectacles sat with a slight list to one side of his nose. The top button of his shirt was undone and his sleeves rolled up to the elbow. He seemed rather tense, or nervous, as he shifted from foot to foot.

"Yes?" His gaze darted from us to the pie and then over the tops of our heads to the road beyond.

"I'm Sam Kostas, Ricky worked in my bakery. We're so sorry for your loss. This is my friend, Grace Devine." Sam pulled the pie from its sling and balanced it on one hand. "I made you a pie. It's steak and kidney." She added when his fingers curled around the wood and he made no sign of moving.

"We won't take up too much of your time. But we'd love to talk to someone about what a lovely chap Ricky was. Were you at the funeral?" I said.

He snorted and pushed his spectacles up his nose, which corrected their lean. "I didn't go to the funeral. I had to work. But I do like a bit of steak and kidney, so I suppose you better come in. I'm Arthur Shadbolt." He took the pie from Sam. Then uttered a soft curse as his palm touched the still-warm bottom. He changed hands and shook the other, which had a narrow crepe bandage tied over the palm.

"Have you hurt your hand?" I asked and then kicked myself for the rather obvious question. People don't bandage their hands because they are bored.

"Oh. Yes. I can be a bit clumsy." He dropped the hand to his and stood aside to let us enter.

Once over the threshold, we followed him down the hall to the kitchen, where the square table was covered in books and papers.

He placed the pie on the bench and took down a plate from the open shelf above. Then Mr Shadbolt carved out a slice of the still-warm pie. "I hope you ladies don't mind, but I haven't had dinner yet."

"Oh, go ahead. It's better eaten straight from the oven. Why don't I make tea?" Sam offered.

He waved to the stove. I filled the kettle and set it to boil, while Sam opened cupboards to find the teapot and the mugs.

"Were you a relative of Ricky's?" I asked. Perhaps the two men were cousins.

He shook his head and didn't reply until he swallowed his mouthful of pie. "He flatted here. I've already had the police here, you know, stomping around and asking lots of questions. But I knew not to say anything to them. You don't have to answer them, you know."

That rather depended on who asked the questions, I thought. Detective Archer had a manner that made me want to blurt out all sorts of confessions. While we waited for the kettle to whistle and out of curiosity, I glanced at the titles of the books spread over the red check tablecloth. One was something about torts, as opposed to tarts. So not a recipe book. Another appeared to be legislation with tightly worded provisions.

Seeing my interest, he gestured to the books with the fork. "I'm studying law. Bloody war interrupted my degree, and I'm picking it back up. Pardon my language," he added as an afterthought.

War interrupted all our lives. Or ended it for many. "It's quite all right, Mr Shadbolt. I think we have all referred to the war as far worse than the rather accurate *bloody*. Is it difficult settling back into your studies?"

He took another swipe through the pie with the fork, it paused halfway to his mouth. "Last year was tough. But things should be easier now."

Sam made a pot of tea. "Shall we go through to the lounge, so we don't disturb your study in here?"

"Right. Good idea. I'd hate to lose my place in that fat tome, took me ages to find the provision I need for my essay. This way." He led us out one door and into the next. The square lounge occupied the front of the house and the lights cast a yellow tinge over the brown leather sofa and chairs.

"I can't imagine how difficult it must be to study the law. What has changed to make it somewhat easier for you now?" I took a seat on the sofa, angled to face the cold fireplace.

Mr Shadbolt dropped to the armchair and balanced his plate on the wide arm. Then he ran a hand through his hair until he tugged on the end. A nervous habit, I thought. "It was Ricky, you see. Coming and going at all times of the night. Kept waking me up. And playing that horrendous music with its caterwauling." He gestured to the phonograph player on its stand under the window.

"That's the nature of working in a bakery, sadly. Everyone wants fresh bread for breakfast, but that takes us hours. We have to be up before the sparrows to set the yeast to activate, and bread must rise before we place it in the oven." Sam placed the tray on the low table and poured. She dropped a lump of sugar into the cup for Mr Shadbolt. Then she regarded him with a narrowed gaze before adding two more.

"It was more than that. Sometimes he had only come home for an hour or so before he left for work again. He never bothered going to sleep when he did, and would play his records while he had a bath, got changed, and headed out again." Mr Shadbolt slurped his tea, before returning to the pie.

Good grief, how had Ricky managed to keep up a chirpy disposition if he didn't sleep the night before work?

I glanced at Sam, who pursed her lips in thought. "I

assume Ricky must have slept as soon as he got off work. Then had his fun in the evening before cycling to the bakery. Not how I prefer to do things, but each to their own."

I couldn't imagine keeping up such a routine. But then I liked to curl up in bed with a book or my sketch pad when darkness fell and was something of a home-body. As Frank and his brother before him used to tease me. Partying and drinking in bars had never appealed much, except on the rare occasion.

Having polished off his pie, Arthur leaned back in the armchair to sip his tea. You could practically see the hot, sweet brew working its magic on him as some of his worries seeped away.

"Do you rent this cottage?" I cast around for a topic of conversation to fill the lull, and to ferret out more nuggets about his relationship with his flatmate.

"Yes, from my parents, who own it. They used to live here, but they moved round the bay while I was at war. When I came back, they said I could rent it from them. It's not easy being a student though, and I need some cash coming in to live on. Foolishly, I thought Ricky would be a fine flatmate. Someone to pay half the expenses, but living his own life without getting involved in mine." He stared into his mug and a line furrowed his forehead.

"Did you tell Ricky that his late-night activities were disturbing you?" It would be hard to live with someone with such a different routine from you. I imag-ined how we would juggle our routines if I shared a home with Sam, but she wouldn't play loud music at three in the morning. Just as I would never disturb her sleep when she toddled off to bed early.

Arthur scoffed and rolled his eyes. "Yes. Repeatedly. He just laughed at me and called me a fuddy-duddy. Damn hard to be alert for early tutorials when he had been keeping me awake for hours."

Curiosity nibbled at me, to know what so offended Mr Shadbolt about Ricky's taste in music. I set my teacup on the table so I could inspect the records stacked in an empty beer crate on the floor. It appeared Ricky had a taste for the new jazz music with its rapid staccato beat. I could imagine that suddenly starting up at three in the morning would be rather a rude awakening.

"I'm sorry he turned out to be such a nuisance. Could you not have asked him to find other accommodation?" The idea of flatting with a stranger seemed a fraught prospect to me. How were differences resolved if you found yourselves incompatible? Although it would be easier to part ways than if you were married. I twisted the ring on my finger as I rose to my feet again, imagining a future that never came to pass.

"Ricky proved as stubborn to remove as a barnacle. I had to give him notice. I can't afford to fail my exams, and I'd do anything for a peaceful night." His words became sharp, and the teacup rattled on its saucer.

Chapter Seven

THE ATMOSPHERE GREW tense and Sam and I exchanged looks.

"Did Ricky find somewhere else to live?" Sam asked.

Mr Shadbolt shrugged. "No idea, but I doubt it, as there aren't any signs of him packing. I was on my last wit, wondering what on earth I could do about him, until..."

Until the problem resolved itself.

"Could we see his room before we go?" The most likely place to find some clue about Ricky's private life would be the room where he spent his most intimate and vulnerable moments. Who knew what we might find shoved under his mattress or in the rubbish bin? I hoped for a threatening letter with a clear and recognisable signature that the police had overlooked.

"If you must. Watch out for his rat." Mr Shadbolt

poured himself another mug of tea and added three sugars before giving it a lazy stir.

"Rat?" I wasn't so sure I wanted to go poking around in his room if a rat lurked in the shadows.

Even brave Sam wrinkled her nose, but she had a personal vendetta against the rodents, as no owner of an establishment selling food wanted a rat scuttling past their customers.

"Ricky kept a pet. Looks like a rat to me. Who is supposed to look after it now? Those coppers weren't much help at all." He gestured to a bedroom across the hall. "It's in there. Hopefully, it's still in its cage and hasn't gnawed through the bars."

Curiosity made us venture into Ricky's room, but I made Sam go first. As Sam flicked on the overhead light, a squeak came from the desk. In a small wire cage with a bit of torn paper on the bottom, crouched a shaggy brown and white creature.

"It's a hamster," I admit to a teeny feeling of relief that while still a rodent, it wasn't the dreaded rat. When I moved closer, the animal wrinkled its nose and pressed itself to the bars. When I reached out a finger, it nibbled at the pad. "Poor thing is hungry. When was it last fed?"

"That Maori copper made me fetch a carrot for it when they came last week." Mr Shadbolt stood in the doorway, his arms crossed.

That Maori copper was most likely Detective Archer. Why had he bothered to find something for the hamster to eat? A part of me whispered because he notices the little things. That was probably what made him a good detective. If there was any evidence in the room that indicated someone other than Harry stabbed Ricky in the back, Detective Archer had probably already found it.

"Has it been fed this week?" Given how the hamster tried to munch on my finger, I doubted the little thing had received any veggies since Detective Archer called.

Mr Shadbolt shrugged. "It's not my problem, is it? I should just let it go out back and it can fend for itself. If it dies in here, it will cause an awful stink." He made a move into the room.

What a horrid thing to suggest. I didn't know much about the natural habitat of hamsters, but I doubted it would last long in the bush with cats and rats. I stepped in front of the desk and made a decision. I picked up the cage and held it close, which resulted in the hamster trying to pull the fabric of my blouse through the wires. "I'll take it. My son can care for it until we can contact Ricky's mother to ask if she wants to collect it. Does it have a name?"

Mr Shadbolt's brows lowered. "Not that I'm aware of. Now if you don't mind, I have quite a bit of study to get through before an exam this week. But thank you for the pie."

He ushered us to the door, and it slammed as soon as we exited his home.

"Odd character," Sam said on the walk back home.

We had learned little, other than law students

appeared a tad highly strung to me. "Yes. He seemed rather annoyed by Ricky's night-time activities. Where do you think he was going, that he didn't get in until nearly start time at the bakery?"

Sam pursed her lips and shook her head. "No idea. He never gave any indication of a wild life after the sun went down. Did you touch Arthur and see anything?"

My gift, if I could call it that, couldn't be turned off and on like a faucet. "No. You don't think he could have done it, do you?"

Her dark eyebrows shot up, and her eyes contained a wealth of experience mine lacked. "I've known men to get into fights about far less than an interrupted night's sleep, the fear of failing final exams, and a flatmate who won't move out. He seemed rather on edge."

"Perhaps he just needs a nice relaxing holiday." That made a thought strike me as we neared our road. "We didn't ask Mr Shadbolt if he went to the beach that Saturday."

Laughter came from Sam. "He didn't strike me as the sort to lie on a towel at the beach."

"Perhaps not. But he might have been the sort to sit in the shade and read a book. Most likely some heavy law text or other." Or like another sort of chap who took a motorcar wearing a three-piece suit to the beach and surveyed the swimming suit clad crowd. Mentally, I picked up a broom and swept a certain detective from my mind.

Sam stopped at her cottage and placed a hand on

the white picket fence. "We are no closer to clearing Harry."

A heaviness settled over me. I knew what I had to do. "I'll talk to Frank, see if he can shed any light on Ricky's nighttime shenanigans."

"Tread carefully. And thank you." She kissed my cheek and waved as she trotted up her path.

Tread carefully. That could be my personal motto. A slight change to *treadle carefully*, and it also encompassed my work life and appeasing the Singer.

I found a carrot for the hamster and gave it fresh water. Then I placed the cage on the small table beside Dad's favourite chair and retired for the night. Once in my nightgown, I grabbed my sketch pad, propping it up on the blankets and against my knees. As I had done with Agatha's murder, I began sketching.

In the middle of my page, I wrote Ricky and drew his laughing face. To one side, I placed Harry's name and a drawing of him clutching a book. Under him went details of his argument with Ricky on the beach that day. On the other side of the page went Mr Arthur Shadbolt. I tapped the pencil against my chin as I considered our visit with him. Then I wrote, angry about being kept awake.

In another corner, I drew a circle and placed in it the odd memory from Ricky as he exited the toilet. The words had pressed on his mind with their mention of being a traitor. Neither Harry nor Arthur matched the voice from that encounter. Someone else had been angry at him, but who and why?

Sam was right. We needed information from the one source who knew more about the underbelly of Wellington than anyone—Frank.

The next morning, Theo was delighted to find the hamster perched on a stool by the table. Dad raised his eyebrows but accepted the new addition to the family. "Why don't we clean out its cage? I've got some fresh sawdust it might like."

I had been too tired last night to do much more than see to the little animal's immediate needs. Now we turned the family's full attention to pampering. Theo cradled it in his hands while I scooped the smelly paper from the cage. As I carried the scraps to the bin, my attention studied the pattern on the paper. Not a pattern, words. Handwritten words. This wasn't newspaper shredded for the hamster, but letters.

My feet slowed as a word and most of its companion leapt out at me...STAY AW...

The tear had amputated the second word and only what could have been the bottom half of the letter *a* came next. Could this be the clue I hoped we might find, but overlooked by the police? What could the torn word be that accompanied *stay* and started with *awa*? It could be stay awake, so he wasn't late for work. Or stay away.

Instead of tossing the slivers away, I found a shallow bowl and piled them inside. With a fingertip, I turned them over. There seemed to be two different pens used, one a blue so dark it was nearly black and a more vibrant blue. From the shapes of the letters I made out, the hand that formed them was different, too. From that, I gathered that at least two letters had been torn up to line the cage. Another squiggle seemed eerily familiar. An *n* followed by an *e* and... was that a *y* or a crooked *l*? Oh, wait. Perhaps it was *nel*? Nelson? My brain tried to solve it like a crossword.

Dad returned with a container of sawdust and shook his head at me as I sat at the table, staring at the pieces of paper. "If you can't bear to throw that lot in the rubbish, we can use that to start the fire. Just pop it in the kindling box."

"No!" I swept the bowl closer to me and hovered over the contents. "I think these are shredded letters to Ricky. I want to see if I can piece them back together."

"Bit of a challenging jigsaw puzzle, if you ask me. The hamster has probably chewed some of your words away." Dad tipped the sawdust into the cage and the fresh fragrance filled the kitchen.

"You never know until you try," I repeated one of Dad's favourite sayings. All I needed was a large amount of patience, a board to smooth the pieces over, and a dash of luck that the hamster didn't eat a pivotal phrase.

"Come on, lad. Let's put him back in here. Then wash your hands and have your breakfast. This after-noon you can help me start a new cage for him." Dad held the cage door open, and Theo placed the hamster on its new bedding.

"He will need a name, too," I said. Apparently, Dad had decided it was a he, although how one could tell I had no idea.

Theo washed his hands in the sink, and his face screwed up in concentration. "Triumph," he said when he returned to the table.

Dad and I shared a smile. The name was no doubt in honour of Theo's favourite motorcycle and the one his uncle rode.

Over breakfast, Dad immediately began sketching plans for a hutch for the animal, so it could enjoy the sunshine and grass in the backyard in finer weather and during the day. While I appreciated him throwing himself into the new housing for the hamster, I itched to have my space finished.

"Don't worry, love, I can sort out your new work-space and build a mighty structure for Triumph. And a hamster with a name like that will probably also need a race car." Dad winked over the rim of his coffee mug at my worried expression. "I will need some lads to move the pieces for the new cutting table, and I'll put it together once it's up those stairs."

Theo refused to be separated from Triumph, who accompanied him to the childminder. The poor thing had gone from being abandoned in an empty room to half a dozen over-excited kids wanting to pet it. I only hoped it survived the experience.

"I'll make sure they give the poor thing a rest and

some quiet time," Mrs Rogers reassured me before I waved goodbye.

Once in the shop's quiet, I plucked the telephone from the counter and pressed the lever to speak to the operator. She connected me to Frank's flat in Mount Victoria. I fully expected to leave a message with his housekeeper. To my surprise, a sleepy voice answered the telephone.

"Hullo?"

My breath hitched. He sounded so like his brother. "Frank, it's Grace."

"Gracie. There's a voice I'd like to wake up to more often." His tone turned from sleepy to something darker that sent a shiver down my spine and was nothing like that evoked by his brother, Freddie.

My fingers tightened on the base of the candlestick telephone. Before my overactive imagination took hold, I blurted out my question. "I need your help with something, if you have time one afternoon?"

Silence fell apart from the odd crackle on the line. The railway clock on my wall ticked the passing seconds while I waited for Frank to consider my request.

"Dinner?"

One word and a simple question. But it concealed so many layers. There needed to be an exchange. He would give his knowledge in return for my companionship. Accepting his proposition also meant another step closer to him and his journey along a shadowy path. Frank made no secret of his desire to make me *his*

Mrs Devine, as opposed to being his dead brother's widow.

And yet...I couldn't think straight when it came to the Devine brothers. Even after six years, memories of Freddie coloured my responses. My brain knew that while the two looked similar, they were chalk and cheese in personalities. Frank would be constant, whereas Freddie was fickle. I already knew his kisses could make my pulse race. But my heart remained to be convinced that accepting Frank fully into my life was a good idea.

"Yes." My need to dig deeper into Ricky's life overcame any reservations.

"I'll pick you up tonight at 6.30."

We said our goodbyes, and I hung the receiver back on its cradle. For some reason, my palms were moist, and I wiped them down the front of my apron.

The turmoil in my mind was soothed by work, placing pins in fabric, and concentrating on one tiny stitch after another. Etty and I made steady progress and squeezed in three fittings during our busy day. The muted chime of four made me look up from the armchair. A hem in delicate and temperamental silk had absorbed my attention.

"You go, Etty. I'll finish this hem and be done for today."

"I'll tidy away, first." My industrious assistant put away her work before covering the dress forms once more and wheeling them into the shadows. She had swept and cleared the table by the time I finished off my piece of thread and snipped as close to the silk as I dared.

Once home, I changed my plain black dress into one with a striped pattern for dinner with Frank. Dad raised his eyebrows, but reserved comment. Rain fell outside, and I peered out the lounge window to spot Frank. I told myself it was to save him from running inside through the horrid weather, but part of it was to save the frosty atmosphere when he waltzed into the cottage without knocking. The temperature had dropped enough without *that* as well.

On Courtney Place, Frank held the umbrella and sheltered us from the rain as we dashed to the restaurant. The waiter pulled the door open as we tumbled inside. Closing the umbrella, Frank stuck his long arm out the doorway to give it a good shake over the pavement. Only then did the door close and leave the blast of foul weather outside.

"Mr Devine." The waiter smiled and gestured to a small table near the back of the restaurant.

We had dined here before, and Frank had some sort of business relationship with the owner. I didn't dig too deep into how he earned his living for fear of what I would uncover.

"What will it be, Gracie?" Frank glanced at me over the top of his menu.

The Italian dishes were a treat, and so different from the meals we cooked at home. I liked to try something new, so I could tell Theo about it over breakfast.

One dish called my name. "The pan-fried scallops." I'd never had them over pasta and it sounded delicious.

An evening with Frank always expanded my experiences. I just hoped I could restrict them to culinary ones tonight.

Chapter Eight

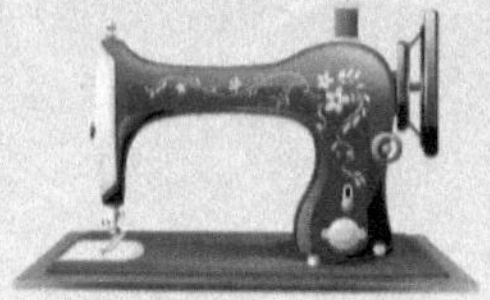

OVER DINNER, we chatted about Theo, my business, and the upcoming royal visit. With his usual patience, Frank waited until I was ready to make my request. Eventually, I steered the conversation in the necessary direction. Frank had his ear to the ground and was a valuable source of information. "Did you know Ricky Hammond?"

Frank sipped his wine and cast me a quizzical look. "No. Is he the chap that got stabbed at the beach?"

"That's him. He worked in the Kostas Bakery, the one run by Sam and her mother." I smoothed the rolled edge of my napkin with a fingertip.

"Why are you asking?" His amber eyes narrowed as he appraised me.

Why indeed? As a favour to Sam, mainly. While I liked Harry, I wasn't entirely sure about him, even if I couldn't imagine a librarian doing such a thing. Someone had obviously plunged a knife into Ricky's back, and there didn't seem to be any other likely suspects. His flatmate, Arthur Shadbolt, was a slim possibility. But that assumed he had been at the bay that Saturday.

Everybody had liked Ricky. But then I thought everybody had liked Agatha, too. That experience should have taught me you never knew what lurked under a smiling facade. Rather like an inviting creek on a summer's day could hide eels in its depths.

"I knew him, and can't imagine anyone wanting to kill him." I had declined a wine and sipped an apple juice. Being around Frank made me want to keep a clear head.

Frank huffed. "And I bet you don't trust that detective to find out who was responsible. I'll ask around and find out what crowd he ran with, and if anyone had a grudge against him."

"His flatmate said he was out late most nights. Apparently, Ricky only came home to bathe and change clothes before heading to work at the bakery. Would you be able to find out where he was going until the early hours?" If anyone knew of clubs open all night during the week and who frequented them regularly, it would be Frank.

With a grin, he saluted me. "How is your dad going with the renovations? You know I can supply a few good lads if you want the job done quickly."

"It's going slowly, but we are edging closer to the finish line. Dad is a perfectionist, and I found him one day using a level to ensure he had all the doors sanded back the same. I can't wait to see it all completed, but wouldn't dare suggest to Dad that I employ someone else to do it, no matter how long it would take him." Dad loved fussing with the new space and building the cabinetry and shelves needed. His attention to detail and craftsmanship would give my little atelier the same feeling of quality and luxury as a haute couture house in Paris. Albeit in a much smaller, and on an antipodean, scale.

As usual, when we neared the end of our meal, Frank slipped away to talk to the owner out back as dessert was served. The routine continued as I never saw him pay for the meal, nor did I ask what business he conducted at the restaurant. Some might think me wilfully blind to what was obviously some sort of off-book transactions taking place. But I preferred to think I protected myself from what I wasn't yet ready to know.

But one day...I would lay a hand on Frank and see if my gift revealed his dark secrets.

He drove me home, parking the Ford on Bowen Street where he had room to manoeuvre the vehicle to head back to his flat. Then he unfolded his lanky form and opened the door for me. Arm in arm, we walked along to Ascot Street and up to my cottage.

I paused at the gate, my hand on the white picket fence Dad had made. "I'll sneak in. It looks like everyone is asleep."

Frank scoffed and shook his head. "It's not even ten, Gracie. A young woman like you should be out enjoying life, not huddled in bed early like a nana. The right man would have you spinning across the dance floor until the wee small hours."

I wouldn't be at all surprised if a seventy-year-old nana sat inside me, clutching her knitting. Besides, I rather enjoyed snuggling in bed, but if I blurted that out, Frank might take it as an invitation to join me. We all grew up fast when war broke out. At the grand old age of twenty-five, I had a child and a business. Both required me to be responsible. Frank had no such concerns.

"Neither Theo nor work will wait in the morning. I hate to think what my stitches would look like if I had only just dragged myself in from a night of dancing." A teeny tiny part of me did sigh at the idea of having fun until dawn in a glorious gown of my own creation. But even Cinderella, who danced with her prince in a palace, still had chores to do in the morning.

Frank kept hold of my hand and drew me closer to him for a kiss. As his arms tightened around me, I placed both hands on his chest and gave him a gentle push. His actions pulled me along a path I wasn't certain I wanted to walk. "Thank you for dinner, Frank, and for your help with Ricky Hammond. Will we see you at the weekend?" I added when hurt flashed in his amber eyes.

"I'll see if I'm free," his tone chilled. With a nod, he turned and strode back to his motorcar.

"Blast," I whispered to myself as I walked down the narrow space at the side of our cottage to the backdoor.

I didn't need my gift to see that a confrontation was brewing with Frank. One day, I would have to be honest with him about my feelings. If only I had resisted charming Freddie all those years ago at the local dance and stayed beside Frank. Would I still be in this pickle, or happily married to the younger brother?

Pondering what my life might have been like occupied my mind until I was burrowed under the blankets and took the hand of sleep for our nightly dance.

Wednesday dawned grey and overcast, and the rain had set in by early afternoon. As a consequence, I had a damp walk home after work. To warm up, I made a cup of hot cocoa and took it to sit by the window, while Theo played on the rug with his toy racing cars. I dragged the armchair around so I could stare at the grey day and curled up with my stocking-clad feet under me. The windowsill was wide enough to serve as a cup holder as I watched the summer rain hitting the glass. The radio played quiet jazz, and I hummed along as my mind turned to Ricky's death and what little Sam and I had uncovered so far. The only people who seemed angry enough to harm him were Harry and Arthur.

Focusing on one fat raindrop that followed a crooked path, I replayed the visit to the cottage and Arthur's burst of anger at how Ricky kept him awake all night and interrupted his study. The way he changed hands holding the pie because one had a strip of bandage over it. Someone else had a cut hand…but who?

To jog my memory, I considered how you could cut your hand. Shaving, if you were particularly bad at it. Scissors, which was why I always handled mine with care. Running a sheet of paper over your skin gave a nasty cut. Or picking up broken glass.

"The waiter!" I sat upright so fast I bumped my nose on the wood of the sill.

That fatal day at the beach, Sam and I had stood on the verandah to wait for ice cream. I had stared into the restaurant of the Pavilion and witnessed a patron berating a waiter for dropping a glass of wine. The server had wrapped a napkin across his palm and the brilliant white was stained with the bright red patch.

The unknown waiter had cut the same palm as Arthur.

I dropped back into the armchair. A coincidence, surely? I pulled what details I could from my memory. The waiter had his back to me and from my obscured view, it was impossible to pick out any distinguishing features. Nor was Arthur particularly remarkable in his construction. The waiter could have been him, or any other man of average build in Wellington. There would be a way to find out. Perhaps another diner at the restaurant who might remember the kerfuffle?

Like Mrs Taylor, who had been on her way to get changed and meet her son. Would he have remarked upon the incident when she took her seat? From memory, my client was due to come in the next day to discuss sketches. She must have known Ricky since she had attended his funeral. Her presence as he was laid to rest gave me an opening to turn the conversation to that day at the beach.

I needed to share the discovery with Sam. As soon as the rain let up, I hurried next door and burst into their cosy kitchen before the clouds shook out more of the wet stuff.

"Hello, Grace. How are you this wet afternoon?" Mrs Kostas sat at the kitchen table with a ledger open before her and a delicious aroma wafted from their large oven.

"A bit damp, thank you, Mrs Kostas. Is Sam around?" I glanced through the next doorway to their lounge.

Sam's mum smiled and gestured over her shoulder. "In there with a book. I like to go over the accounts in here. It seems more business-like to sit at the table." She winked at me and chuckled.

Sam sat in the gloomy lounge, a book resting on her chest as she stared out the window.

"You'll ruin your eyesight reading on a day like this without a light on," I scolded her.

Sam closed the book and patted the sofa next to her. "I'm not that interested in the novel, anyway. I just wanted to give Mum some peace while dinner cooks and she does the books. Hopefully, she doesn't cook the books."

I dropped to the worn velvet seat and leaned against my friend. "Do you remember that when we visited Arthur Shadbolt, he had a bandage on his palm?"

"Yes. Why is this news?" Interest shone in her dark eyes.

I took a breath and let out my suspicion. "That morning at the beach, I remember peering into the restaurant when a waiter cut his hand on a broken glass. The same palm as the injury on Arthur. What if the waiter was him? That would put Arthur at Days Bay, meaning he might have had the opportunity to stab Ricky."

Sam screwed up her face. "You're stretching it a bit. But he seemed the angry sort with a short fuse."

"And he seemed rather miffed that Ricky and his music were interrupting his studies. How could we find out if he was the waiter?" Two heads were better than one, and I couldn't fill in the missing pieces without Sam's help. I could knock on Arthur's door and ask, but how could I trust any answer he gave? Killers were seldom truthful about their whereabouts.

A soft humming came from Sam as she pondered the question. "Let me talk to Estelle. Chefs gossip like fishwives and she might know someone who works in the kitchens at the Pavilion. The waiters and kitchen staff all know each other and we might have a source who handled the...sauce."

I groaned at her attempt at a culinary joke. That one was worse than the subtle *cooking the books*. "Stick to making bread."

"You mean keep making dough?" When I maintained my silence, she snorted. "Ok, I admit those are bad, but I couldn't let the opportunity pass. I'll be serious now." She mimed buttoning up her lips, but her eyes shone with mischief.

I wondered how long she had been saving the terrible jokes. "You're lucky I love you and that you are the most amazing baker. Please see if Estelle can help. I'll drop a few hints around Joseph and see what he knows." The clock on the mantel gave a ding for the half-hour and reminded me I had two fellows who would want dinner shortly. "I better rustle up something for my troops."

After leaving the Kostas cottage, I trotted through the drizzle to our home and along the path to the workshop. As luck would have it, Joseph was in the workshop with Dad and Theo. The three of them were clustered around the workbench, staring at the lathe. Joseph held Theo up to watch as Dad finished turning what looked like a table leg.

I tapped Joseph on the shoulder as he put Theo down. "Can I have a quick word?"

A wary edge crept over his face. "What about?"

I pulled him to one side of the workshop and away from Theo's ears. "Richard Hammond. His flatmate, Arthur Shadbolt, has a cut palm. Do you know how he did it?"

Joseph's broad shoulders heaved in a deep sigh. "Do you think Detective Archer missed that? Shadbolt said he dropped a plate and cut himself picking up the pieces."

I should have known the detective would have spotted the bandage and questioned Arthur about how he acquired the wound. The law student certainly gave a plausible story. Or he might have cut himself when he fumbled a customer's glass in the Pavilion. "Did Detective Archer ask where he was that Saturday?"

Joseph didn't answer. He folded his arms and gave me a look probably not that dissimilar from the one I gave Sam when she tried her terrible word puns. So he had asked. "And? Was he at Days Bay? You can stand there and stare at me, but I'm not giving up. You may as well answer my question, or I'm going to invite myself to tea with Mrs Cox every night."

He closed his eyes for a moment and they rolled behind his lids. No doubt he was imagining what I would tell his landlady. "No, he wasn't there. Said he was writing some paper that was due on Monday."

I patted Joseph's arm. "Thank you. That's all I needed to know."

My cousin left for his own dinner, and I reminded Theo to go and wash up. My feet moved at a slower pace along the path to the house. I had been so certain Arthur must be involved and cut his palm wielding the knife. But if he wasn't there, it had to be someone else.

Unless he had lied to the detective.

Chapter Nine

THURSDAY NIGHT and with nowhere else to be, I tackled what Dad referred to as my hamster puzzle. After considering how best to approach the scrunched-up and narrow strips, I treated them as though they were wrinkled fabric. I couldn't begin trying to stick them back together until they were flattened. The easiest way to achieve that was with a piece of equipment every seamstress was familiar with—the iron.

I spent a quiet evening heating the iron on the stove, and carefully passing the heavy metal over each tiny scrap. A folded tea towel stopped them from burning, and after an hour I had a neat stack of strips. Next, I fetched a sheet of cardboard and my pin cushion.

"Are you branching out into hamster fashion? Or disposable paper-wear?" Dad followed my activities over the top of his book.

"Don't jest about hamster fashion, or Theo will

want a scarf and goggles for when you make a race car for his new friend." Although Triumph would look fabulous with a bright blue scarf tossed around his neck. I could easily knit one with a leftover skein of yarn.

Before I got distracted by knitting a scarf for the rodent, I drew my attention back to the litter from the bottom of his cage. I had separated the pieces out by the ink used on them. Dark navy went in one pile, a pale blue in another. The pale blue pile was far larger and seemed more like a letter. The dark navy was possibly a quickly dashed note.

Finally, I was ready to discover the rest of the word that had first caught my eye. With the board in front of me and the basket of scraps to one side, I picked up the strip that inspired the somewhat daft task and skewered it to the middle of the board.

STAY AW...

"What could you be?" I asked the partial word. My best guess was AWAKE. Someone who worked in a bakery and had to get up before the sparrows would need to stay awake when they had been out all night. Ricky might have been the sort of person who left himself notes. I examined each bit of paper looking for a capital AKE.

I found another capital A, but it was followed by a Y. I compared it to my starting point and the torn edge matched. A pin at each end secured the sliver to the board and revealed the phrase...STAY AWAY...

That was a lot more interesting than a reminder to

stay awake. "What did you need to stay away from, Ricky? Or who?"

I sorted through the other scraps to reveal the rest of the message. The radio played music, and I hummed to myself as I picked up, compared, and discarded strips in the same manner as if I were completing a jigsaw puzzle. When one piece fitted, I pinned it in place with as much care as though I was beading lace. Some lines were torn in half, and I matched the top half of the words to the bottom.

The note came together quickly with its few lines and angry-looking letters. Someone had pressed so firmly upon the paper the nib of his pen nearly went all the way through. It didn't take too long before I had most of it (minus a few chewed corners) put back together.

> *You might think her old and foolish*
> *but you'll never see a penny*
> *STAY AWAY*
> *from my mother*
> *Or else*
> *I'll be watching you*

"Oh, Ricky," I whispered. The note implied he had been trying to obtain cash from someone's mother. Blackmail, perhaps? Could whoever penned the note have delivered the 'or else' consequences he warned of, when Ricky didn't stop?

I hadn't known Ricky that well and thought of him

as the handsome and charming fellow who worked behind the counter in a bakery. But people's lives were like onions. You peeled away one layer to discover another. What would I find when I finally pulled back the last layer of his life?

Mid-morning Saturday, Sam stuck her head in our back door and grinned at me. "You free for lunch?"

I glanced around at the empty kitchen. "Yes. I find myself all alone and with no one else to consider today. Theo has gone to play at a friend's house, and I'll collect him later this afternoon. Dad and Joseph are moving a large cabinet into the shop for me, and I'm not allowed to peek, apparently." To keep myself away, and not in the mood to sketch, I worked on the torn strips of paper from the hamster cage, slowly assembling the letter that seemed to be more of a general chatty update such as an elderly aunt might send about whom she saw walk past her window.

"Grab your hat and bag, then. We're meeting Estelle up at the Arms. She has news from a friend who works at the Pavilion." She entered the cosy kitchen and leaned on the counter.

"Oh! Brilliant." I put the board away, along with the flattened shreds waiting to be matched up and fetched my bag.

Arm in arm, we took the path to our local pub. Inside was quiet, with only a scattering of people having quiet conversations and one person sitting at the bar doing a crossword. We headed for our usual corner table. Estelle Mersey sat there already and gave us a cheerful wave as we approached. Estelle was a chef who had provided a useful piece of information when we had searched for who killed Agatha Marshall. Her dark hair was cropped short and brushed against her ears.

"Oh, I love your new hairstyle," I said as I sat down. The last time we had met, her dark curly hair had been gathered at her nape in a large bun.

She bounced the curled edge on her hand. "Do you like it? I felt like a change."

"It suits you. I'm thinking about going shorter myself." Hairstyles were heading in the same direction as hemlines. Long hair pinned to look short was the rage among some, but it took time and effort. I was tempted to lop mine off as Estelle had. It's funny how I easily adopted the hottest trends in fashion, but my hand shook if I tried to take the shears to my hair.

"You should do it, too. Some women go even shorter with the new bob style," Estelle said.

"Perhaps I will." If we had a quiet moment in the shop on Monday, I might get Etty to cut my hair. It would certainly free up time in the morning, not having to pin it into place anymore.

We ordered lunch and Sam fetched our drinks from the bar. She placed one in front of me and glanced at Estelle. "So...did you find anything out?"

"I asked around. You know I'd do anything to help clear old Harry." Estelle took a sip from her drink.

I only sipped at my drink, needing to know about the mysterious waiter and the altercation. "Sam tells me you know someone who works at the Pavilion."

She nodded and swallowed before replying. "Yes. A mate works in the kitchen on weekends. I asked him about the day Ricky died. He said they were run off their feet with all the people flocking to the beach since it was such a glorious weekend."

The steamer had been crammed full of people that day. The beach was as busy as the restaurant. So many towels were spread over the sand, it looked like a giant patchwork quilt.

"Did your friend remember the waiter who dropped a glass and cut his hand?" While Joseph had told me that Arthur spent the day studying, my curiosity had to know more about the waiter and the angry customer.

"Couldn't forget it. Fred made a comment about the waiter being all thumbs, and that they would never have sent him out into the restaurant if they weren't so short-handed. Then he said he hoped he'd make a better lawyer than he did a waiter."

"What? The waiter was studying to be a lawyer?" I glanced at Sam, not sure if I had heard correctly or if my overactive imagination was filling in connections.

Estelle picked up a fork and tackled her lunch. She kept talking between mouthfuls. "I think Fred said he was a student. Apparently, one of their regular waiters was sick and sent a friend as a last-minute replacement to cover his shift."

"Did your friend remember his name?" My fork stopped halfway to my mouth. I couldn't continue eating my lunch until I heard the answer as impossible as it might be.

Estelle screwed up her face and stared at the ceiling. "Art something? They don't take names or fill out forms with casuals. It's all under-the-table stuff when a regular employee finds their own replacement."

My stomach lurched. Art was short for Arthur. Arthur Shadbolt had been there that day. He didn't cut his hand on a plate, but a glass. Which meant he could have had an argument with Ricky when he took a break. If he wore an apron, it could have been tossed in the laundry with all the others and treated like a red wine or tomato sauce stain.

Sam swore quietly under her breath. "Well, I'll be. That flatmate of Ricky's could have done him in after all."

"He must have seen Ricky down by the wharf, had a row and...perhaps stabbed him with a knife he had grabbed from the kitchen?" In my mind, an angry law student snatched a nearby blade, and stormed off after his housemate who played loud music in the middle of the night and kept him awake.

"We need to confront him and make him go to the police and confess." Sam's hand tightened on her glass.

There was no point wandering the university campus trying to find him. The law student would most likely spend his evenings studying or writing papers that were due for his lecturers. "Shall we pay another visit to his flat?" I suggested.

Sam clenched her jaw. "Yes, and this time he won't be getting a pie."

That evening after dinner, Sam and I once again walked up the steep road to Arthur Shadbolt's cottage. A light blazed in the window and a mix of relief and anxiety churned inside me. I was relieved to find him home, but the idea of the oncoming confrontation made me nervous.

Sam rapped sharply on the door, then stood with her arms crossed.

After a few moments, feet thudded in the hall, and the door opened. Arthur stood there with his shirt sleeves rolled up to his elbows and an open book in his hand. He narrowed his gaze at us. "You two. You're not trying to return that rat, are you?"

A shudder worked through me every time he said the word *rat*. "No, my son is quite fond of Triumph. We'd like to talk to you about something else."

"Well, I am rather busy. I'm studying for exams and don't have time to chat." He lifted the book and made to close the door.

Sam placed a hand on the wood. "We'd like to talk to you about your whereabouts on the day Ricky died."

"I was here, writing a paper, just like I told the

cops." He flicked the book closed and held it before him, but his Adam's apple bobbed up and down.

My friend leaned in closer to the student. "No, you weren't. We happen to know you were working in the restaurant and that's how you cut your hand. But if you don't want to talk to us, we'll go and tell the police that you lied to them."

His tongue wet his lips, and his shoulders heaved. "Come inside and make it quick."

We followed him inside and assembled in the lounge. The coffee table was strewn with books and torn pieces of paper.

"Why did you lie to the detective?" I got my question out before bravery fled me. Personally, I couldn't form an untruth when Detective Archer stared at me, and I wondered how Arthur had managed it. Or maybe murderers find it easier to lie.

"I didn't do it." Arthur ran his hands through his hair and created more of a mess among his unruly locks.

Sam let out a snort. "Come on. How did you think you wouldn't get caught? Everyone remembers you dropping the glass and cutting yourself on a shard."

Arthur tossed his book to a pile, and the whole lot lurched to one side. "I was doing Nigel a favour, and I needed the money. They pay casual staff cash in hand, no need to tell the tax boys. As far as the Pavilion is concerned, I was Nigel for the day. Besides, they were short-staffed and couldn't complain too much about it."

"Did the police ask for your name that day?" I

threaded my quiet questions in between Sam's angrier ones. We were delayed boarding the steamer to return across the bay as the sweating constables had taken everyone's name.

"They didn't ask, just took the roster of who was working that day." Arthur paced back and forth in front of the fireplace.

That supported his claim to be studying all day, as the roster showed his friend had a shift.

"Since you had an alibi all set up, did you go looking for Ricky that morning?" Sam stood beside the coffee table.

Arthur stopped his pacing and stared at us. "No! I'm telling you I didn't kill him. I want to be a lawyer, not a prisoner. Nor did I have any time. We were so busy, we barely got a chance to go to the toilet, and no one had a break. One chap was caught about to pee in a wine carafe, he was that desperate. Did whomever you spoke to at the restaurant tell you that bit?"

Sam and I exchanged looks. I made a note not to drink the wine from a carafe if we ever dined at the Pavilion. But Arthur was right. If the Pavilion was that busy, he wouldn't have had a spare half-hour to sneak away, commit murder, and remove any trace of blood from his clothing.

But if he didn't do it, who did?

Chapter Ten

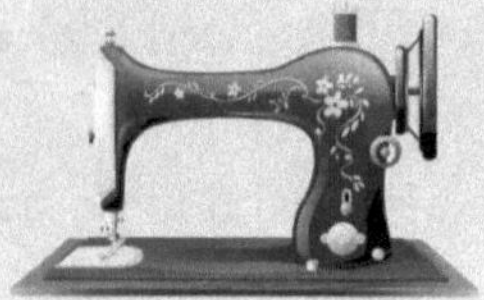

Monday morning, Mrs Taylor entered my shop like a gust of autumn wind, dressed in burnt orange and deep red. We had yet to decide on the final sketch for an evening dress, as nothing I had drawn so far had quite met her expectation. Today, I had four sketches to show her and hoped that one would meet her approval.

"Good morning, Mrs Taylor. You are looking lovely today," I said as I helped her out of her coat and handed it to Etty to hang up. "I have the sketches for you, and I have gone in a slightly different direction this time."

While my shop didn't have much space, we had created a spot where a client could sit in the comfortable armchair, sipping a cup of tea, while I showed them my sketches. As I led Mrs Taylor to the brown Chesterfield with its buttoned back, she paused at my cutting table and glanced at the newspaper sitting in one corner.

I admit to ghoulishly reading any updates on the

death of Richard Hammond and who might be a suspect. Today's edition of The Dominion sat folded open at the latest article.

Mrs Taylor rested her hand over the inked words. "What a terrible tragedy for a bright young life to end in such a manner."

"It is a great loss. Richard was such a cheerful chap. Did you know his family?" I recalled her tearful face at the funeral, hastily hidden by a thick veil. Sam thought she must have been a customer of the bakery, but an association with Mrs Hammond seemed more likely.

"Oh, no. I don't know them at all. But he seems such a handsome smiling chap in all the photographs, don't you think?" She bustled over to the comfortable chair and sat, just as Etty carried out a black tea with a slice of lemon. A homemade gingernut biscuit balanced on the saucer.

Mrs Taylor lied! Why would anyone attend the funeral of a stranger and be that distressed over seeing a photograph in the newspaper? Since it wouldn't do to accuse a marvellous client of telling pork pies and demand the truth, instead I put a smile on my face and grabbed my sketchbook.

Getting back to work, I wheeled over my stool and sat next to my client. We soon lost ourselves in a dream world of sparkling ballrooms and dancing the night away. Briefly, I remembered Frank's words that I should be out enjoying life at night and not curled up in bed. But in my mind, I did stay up until dawn and crept home dangling a pair of heels in one hand. Or was it terribly sad that I lived a high-society life through the wealthy women that I clothed?

"Oh, I do like that one!" Mrs Taylor exclaimed as I turned the page.

The floaty gown was my favourite, with its narrow shape adding height to Mrs Taylor's form. The vertical beading would add to the illusion. "I thought the beads would be like rain trailing down a windowpane." The idea had come to me one day as I watched a storm batter the cottage.

As I handed her the sketch to consider, our hands grazed, and a memory jumped from her mind to mine.

I propped myself up on my elbows on the lush blue velvet coverlet on the enormous bed.

My gorgeous man stalked across the rug towards me, mischief glinting in his eyes. His tie dangling loose around his neck. The top three buttons of his shirt undone to reveal a triangle of dark hair. In one hand, he held a champagne bottle in the other two flutes. 'Well, Lynette, since you have encouraged me to turn over a new leaf and make amends for old ways, what say we do a little celebrating as we embark on our new life?'

'Oh, yes, Ricky.' I uncrossed my legs and the aqua silk of the gown slid to reveal my naked thighs.

Ricky! But...him and Mrs Taylor? No! She was so... old. She must be at least fifty and Ricky closer to half that. I must have been mistaken. Except I had a clear image of his face and she said his name. My memories were always from the perspective of the person I touched. It wasn't like I accidentally saw a glimpse from her maid's mind instead. And he had said, Lynette. That was Mrs Taylor's Christian name. Nor could I mistake the amply-shaped naked legs after the hours we had spent in a fitting room together. A seamstress took all sorts of measurements to ensure the perfect fit of an ensemble.

I coughed, nearly choking on the image and its implications, as I tried to shoo it from my mind.

"Are you quite all right, Grace?" Mrs Taylor asked.

"Yes." I struggled to squeeze the syllable from my throat as it constricted. "I think I swallowed a bug."

Her face screwed up, and she swatted an imaginary one with her hand. Straight after work, I was telling Sam that Mrs Taylor knew Ricky and it had nothing to do with a hot sausage roll. It took a bit of effort to drag my concentration back to the sketches and explaining my vision for each. Etty fetched the swatch book, and I indicated what fabrics and patterns might work with the gowns.

"I thought blues for the raindrop gown. The beads would be a light blue and silver, to give the shimmer of water." I flicked the pages of the swatch book to a selection of pale blues that mimicked a summer sky.

The bell above the door tinkled as a tall and narrow blond man burst into the shop. Hand still on the knob, he glanced at Mrs Taylor. "Are you not done yet, Mummy? It's nearly time for our luncheon reservation."

"Not quite, Karl." Mrs Taylor took another look at

the sketches before tapping the page. "This one, it will be quite daring, will it not?"

Mummy? It was one thing for Theo to call me that...but a grown man? Addressing your mother as Mummy when you were past the age of thirty sounded terribly British, posh, and a little bit royal.

My attention dropped back to the sketchbook. "A bold choice, but you will be a regal presence in this gown, Mrs Taylor."

Quietly, I was pleased with her choice of the raindrop gown. It didn't follow current trends for older women and I hoped, would spark the imagination of potential clients at the event. I darted a look at the newcomer with his rather imperious demands. I assumed he took after his father with his lanky and pale build. I tilted my head and dared a longer look. He looked familiar for some reason.

Then it came to me. Arthur. He had been the man waiting in the restaurant that day at the beach who had yelled at Arthur when he dropped the wine glass. Mrs Taylor and I had been so absorbed in discussing potential gowns that I had forgotten to find another way to ask her about Ricky.

"Did you have a pleasant lunch the day I saw you at Days Bay? I've never eaten in the Pavilion restaurant." I closed the sketchbook and placed my pencil on top.

Before Mrs Taylor could answer, Karl leapt into the conversation. "Some idiot dropped my wine and nearly ruined my trousers. I had to get changed and lucky I had a spare pair in the car. I demanded the restaurant pay for cleaning, of course, and we got our lunch for free. Although they shouldn't hire incompetent waiters like that. It's a marvel someone that clumsy survived the war and didn't drop a grenade on himself."

My eyebrows shot up. "Everybody has a bad day," I murmured. Certainly, I'd seen enough of them and had pushed the needle through my finger when sewing.

"I thought the food was delicious and sent my compliments to the chef," Mrs Taylor countered her son's dour opinion of the restaurant. She rose and Etty held out her coat for her to slip her arms into.

I clutched the sketchbook to my chest. "I will have a mock-up for the fitting in about two weeks." In my head, I estimated how long it would take us to draft the pattern and cut out the muslin gown for the fitting.

Karl wandered around the room and arched an eyebrow at the pattern pieces stacked on one corner of the cutting table. "Really, Mummy, don't you think you have enough silly dresses? What is wrong with wearing a frock you already have? I can't believe this is how you fritter away my inheritance."

Wear an old gown to the grand ball in honour of the Prince of Wales? Mrs Taylor and I exchanged horrified looks.

"This is a special occasion, Karl, and calls for a memorable evening dress." She buttoned up her coat and picked up her handbag.

He snorted, then his critical eye fell to the folded newspaper. "Well, at least I've reined in your spending in *one* department."

Mrs Taylor stilled, and her face paled. "This is neither the time nor the place to discuss how I spend my money, Karl. Mrs Devine is worth every penny and her gowns are much sought after among Wellington high society."

"I have an image to maintain, you know. That motorcar is nearly three years old and not as fast as the new models," he grumbled as they headed towards the door.

The older woman's hands tightened on her handbag. "Perhaps you should consider paid employment if you don't find your allowance sufficient."

Etty held the door open, a bright smile on her face. "Have a lovely day," she called out as they left. Then she turned to me with laughter in her hazel eyes. "Well, that was awkward. But I agree with Mrs Taylor. She can spend her money however she likes and if he feels hard done by, it wouldn't hurt him to dirty his hands with a job."

"Yes." The word came from my distracted mind. I stared down Plimmer Steps, watching the two very different forms hurry towards a waiting motorcar. A pieced-together note floated in my mind's eye.

Stay away from my mother, or else.

Had Karl carried out his threat, and *that* was the area of expenditure he had curbed?

When I got home that afternoon, I was bursting to share with Sam. But first I had to greet Theo and Dad. My men were busy in the workshop constructing a new run for the hamster that included a snug house and ramps. Upstairs, I stripped off my plain black dress and pulled on wide-legged trousers and a light cotton blouse, before hurrying next door.

"Mrs Taylor was having some sort of relationship with Ricky, and I think her son killed him!" I blurted out in a hushed whisper, not wanting Mrs Kostas to overhear.

Sam put down her book and arched one dark brow. Then she pushed a chair out with her foot. "Well, that's quite the development for a Monday. Sit and tell me all. I'll make tea."

The best place to start would be at the beginning, and the first inkling I had that my client knew the murdered man. "Remember we saw Mrs Taylor at the funeral, and your mother thought she might know Ricky's mother?"

Sam made a noise of agreement as she fetched mugs and measured out tea.

"She came into the shop today, as she needed to decide on the final sketch for a gown I am making for her. I had an article about Ricky open on the cutting table, and she made a comment about how sad it was that he died. I asked her if she knew him, and she said no. Which we know is a lie! We saw her sitting there at the back of his funeral." Why did people lie when they were so easily caught out? Like Arthur and cutting his hand. Mrs Taylor must have seen me unless her tears had blurred her vision?

The kettle let out a short puff, and Sam poured boiling water into the pot.

"Then we were sitting there, looking at my sketches and when I passed one to her, our hands touched." I paused then, as Sam carried over the pot in one hand, the mugs dangling from her other.

Sam's eyebrow arched higher. My friend was a master at making that furry black line convey as much as any spoken sentence. I was about to get to the good bit while she poured the tea.

"She was lying on a bed, in a state of undress. Ricky walked towards her holding a bottle of champagne and two glasses and asked if she was ready to celebrate their new life." The words tumbled out in a rush, and I wanted to screw up my eyes to take away the images that accompanied them. "I thought he liked Harry? Why would he be...entertaining Mrs Taylor?"

Both eyebrows shot up, and Sam's eyes widened. Then she let out a near-silent whistle. "Oh, Ricky. Some people are attracted to who a person is on the inside, not who they are on the outside."

I tried to make sense of that. "But aren't we all attracted to who someone is, not their appearance?"

Sam shook her head and smiled at me. "To some, it doesn't matter if they are a man or woman. It's about how that person makes them feel."

Oh. I understood that. For myself, I hadn't decided yet how to interpret the queasy feeling inside that Frank inspired. It could be attraction, nerves, or my body trying to escape the situation. "That still seems unfair to Harry. To lead him along like that, if Ricky was already having a relationship with someone else.

Or that might be why he was being a bit coy with Harry?"

"Or he might have been a gold digger. This must have been what he meant when he said to Harry that he had found someone who would give him life on easy street." Sam drank her tea and leaned back in her chair.

Some people valued security more than love. Mrs Taylor was wealthy and well-connected. She would certainly have been able to give Ricky all the finer things in life. Another memory wound its way through me and left me with a dry throat. "Her son, Karl. He was angry about her spending money on new dresses with me."

Sam huffed. "Why is it any of his concern how she spends her money?"

I took a gulp of tea to moisten the way for what I had to say next. "Then he said that at least he had reined in her spending in one department. And he was looking at the article about Ricky when he said it."

"Is that why you think he did it?" Interest flared in Sam's eyes.

"No, it's because of the note I found in the hamster cage that said, 'Stay away from my mother, or else'."

Chapter Eleven

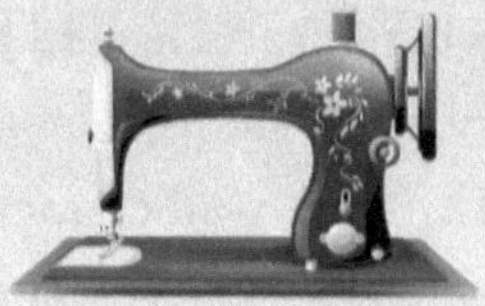

Our eyes met across the table. Sam tapped one blunt fingernail against her mug. "Before we get too excited, where was Karl Taylor that Saturday?"

"In the Pavilion restaurant. He was the one yelling at Arthur for breaking the glass." From what I had seen, Karl had appeared angry and out of sorts. Had he confronted Ricky about his relationship with Mrs Taylor and put an end to her frivolous expenditure?

"I bet more people are killed over money than whatever weak excuse has the police looking at Harry." Sam took a gulp of her tea.

Sam was getting Estelle to ask her friend if Arthur had disappeared at any point during that day, but it now seemed unlikely he ended Ricky's life. "Karl Taylor said he had to change his trousers as he had red wine on them. I wonder how many spare pairs he kept in the trunk of his motor?"

"You need to tell Joseph about Mrs Taylor, Ricky,

and this note. Especially after the comment her son made about curbing her spending." Sam waggled a finger in my direction.

My face flushed red at the mere idea of repeating what I saw in the flash of borrowed memory to my cousin. "I most certainly will not! Besides, I'm sure Detective Archer has already interviewed them."

Sam moved her tea mug to one side so she could reach across the table and take my hand. "People lie, especially when they have something to hide. Like Arthur Shadbolt did. Do you really think Mrs Taylor blurted out the intimate details of her relationship? That's if the police even know about it to question her in the first place."

I opened my mouth to argue and then snapped it shut again. I didn't know about the secret liaison, even after some years of sharing the intimacy of the fitting room with Mrs Taylor. The tense conversation in my shop between mother and son hinted that he had known about it and if he penned the note, that would confirm he knew about the relationship. So wouldn't others have also commented on the older woman being wooed by a much younger, and poorer, man?

I nibbled the rim of the mug as I thought. Such a tasty rumour would fly around that set and there was one person who would catch and keep such informa-tion. Mrs Cooper. Luckily, my mentor was coming in this week to view the new space. I would ask about Mrs Taylor when I had a chance.

Sam shook my hand. "Please, Grace. You have to

talk to Joseph, for Harry. You can't let them stitch him up if there's a chance this Karl Taylor was involved."

Selfishly, I didn't want to lose Mrs Taylor as a client. She challenged me creatively and always paid on time. Fittings would become awkward if I helped put her son in jail for murdering her handsome lover. But Sam was right. I couldn't let the police pin something on Harry when there might be someone else with a far better motive.

I blew a sigh over the surface of my tea. "I'll track Joseph down and ask. Although I am wearing out the number of favours he owes me. He already let loose that Arthur Shadbolt told them he cut his palm on a broken plate."

Sam sat up straighter. "Arthur might prove to be a dead end, but we can still save Harry from a drab prison uniform, or worse, a rope necklace if Kostas and Devine crack this case."

Disbelief erupted from me, and I nearly spat out tea. "Kostas and Devine? Are we opening a new business?"

"We do make a pretty good team." She winked.

We did make a good team, but I didn't want to make sleuthing my main occupation. Once I took on more staff to expand, I doubt I would have time for poking into the lives of other people. Unless they were clients. While my innate sense of justice drove me to find who did snatch Ricky's life, this would be the last time. After all, how many people in my circle of acquaintances could get murdered?

Tuesday afternoon Frank loitered in the shade waiting for me to lock up.

"Hello, Frank," I said as the key twisted in the lock.

"Gracie. Can you spare a little time for a tired old soldier?" He touched the brim of his hat and angled it down to shield his eyes from the late afternoon sun.

I slid my hand through his offered arm. "There is nothing old or tired about you. I would describe you as all charm and irresistible intrigue. And of course I have time for you."

He chuffed a soft laugh. "So there is hope for me, that I might yet find a tiny space in your heart?"

His words cut me. There would always be a place for him in my affections, as the much-loved uncle of Theo. As for something bigger than that... Well, never again would I be the victim of some man's games, such as those one brother had played on another. Nor would I allow one man's secrets to derail the path I now walked.

"You know that you are a much-loved member of our little family unit. Theo adores you and I suspect you are his favourite uncle." A little flattery would soothe his ego and brush away the conversation he tried to initiate.

"Really? He spends so much more time with Joseph." We emerged on Lambton Quay, and he opened the door of his motorcar for me.

"Ah, but Joseph is a policeman. You...are not.

There is a hint of mystery about what exactly you do, and I suspect Theo is convinced you are a spy. While my son is asleep, he dreams that you are off conducting daring missions and on adventures that you cannot tell us about because they are secret." I winked and tapped the side of my nose.

Frank chuckled as he started the Ford and climbed back in. "Favourite, huh?"

His grin warmed my insides, and I melted like chocolate left out in the sun. He was the most striking man when he smiled and the light illuminated those auburn eyes.

"Shall we take a stroll in the gardens?" I wasn't sure what he had planned, but I didn't want to be too long as Theo and Dad expected me home.

"If you'd like. I've done some digging like you asked about that chap." He steered the motorcar along the road and around the corner.

Once he parked the Ford outside the Botanic Gardens, we found an empty park bench and sat facing the fountain. Frank ran his arm along the back of the bench and his body offered protection from the slight breeze. "He was a funny fellow that Hammond. Seemed to spread himself thin across Wellington. Some nights he hung out at a pub up Willis Street called The Scrum and Tackle. That's run by a former rugby player and lads gather there to drink and discuss rugby in winter and cricket over summer. Bit of a rough crowd though, and it's known for more than a few brawls.

Ricky was also rumoured to do a spot of waitering at a classy place on Courtney Place where our sort is turned away at the door. Between those two extremes, he also liked to visit the Cricket."

I tried to reconcile the different sides of Ricky. There was the handsome lad who wooed a wealthy older woman, then the side that downed a pint and argued over rugby. But was there a third side that had given Harry the impression he liked the company of other men for more than talking about sport?

I doubted Harry had met Ricky at a place called The Scrum and Tackle, but I could see the librarian catching the show at the Cricket and chatting at the bar. If Ricky worked at a swanky restaurant, that was most likely where he met Mrs Taylor. I wondered when he had time to sleep with all his late-night and early-morning activities. No wonder his flatmate was tearing his hair out.

"This rugby club, do you know if he had a group of friends there?" We still hadn't completely eliminated Arthur as a suspect, and there was Karl Taylor to consider, but there was no harm in learning if anyone else had argued with Ricky.

Frank screwed up his face. "Yes, but you don't want to get involved with them, Gracie. Leave it alone."

No sooner had he said the words than my brain declared that I would not leave it alone and I would most definitely be poking my nose into their business. "Why, Frank? Who are they?"

He let out a deep exhale and his hand moved to my shoulder. "They call themselves the Bin Men."

"As in the sin bin?" I might not be the closest follower of the sport that obsessed our nation, but the only bin metaphor I knew associated with the game was the sin bin. That was an area where players were sent for bad behaviour and breaking the rules. Rather like sending Theo to sit in a corner and think about what he had done when he was naughty.

"Which is why I don't want you going anywhere near them. They're known for getting into fights."

That didn't seem like the smiling Ricky at all. Why would he be involved with such a rough bunch? "Does this group have a leader?"

Frank let out a sigh. "Geoff Dwyer. He used to be a rugby player. Was quite good and rumoured to make the All Blacks until the war intervened."

"What happened?" Lives and careers were cut short or re-made by the war. Tragic events working like some celestial tailor making a snip here, or a stitch there.

Frank slapped his thigh. "Shrapnel in his legs. Poor bugger can't run anymore. Still throws a heck of a punch though, I hear."

"Why was Ricky part of such a group?" I mused out loud.

A finger under my chin turned my face to Frank. "You're not going to let it go, are you?"

I smiled and pulled his hand down. "No. The

Ricky who worked in the bakery doesn't fit in the group you describe. I need to know why." I also needed a way to get myself into that club without getting myself into trouble. The wind turned colder, and I stood. "I'm going to cut through the track home if you'd like to accompany me?" A path carved through the trees and down towards Bowen Street.

"Of course." Frank tapped his fedora to make sure it sat tighter on his head, then he rose to his full height.

"I suspect that in a few more years, Theo will be as tall as you, and I will need to stand on a chair to tell him off." I took his arm, and we headed for the trees. Soft green boughs draped over the path, and we walked in the dappled light. Under the branches with the earthy aroma of soil, the city could have been a thousand miles away, not on the doorstep.

"Promise me you'll stay away from Dwyer," Frank urged.

"I have a family and business to think of. I can certainly promise that I won't do anything silly." Rushing headlong into trouble with a bayonet fixed to a rifle was for other people. I preferred to consider all the problems in advance. Which meant finding a way to learn more about this Dwyer without getting into his line of sight.

"Good." Frank seemed to find my words enough of a reassurance.

A familiar twittering came from the dense canopy. I made a chirping noise in response, trying to lure the little bird closer. Then it plummeted down from a branch and shot across the path right in front of us before landing on a twig and calling out.

I held out my hand as the cheeky fantail flitted closer and closer to us.

"Hello little *pīwakawaka*," I cooed as its feathers brushed over my palm for a moment before it flew back to safety amongst the greenery.

"Pipi-what?" Frank held back an overhanging branch, a frown pulling his eyebrows closer together.

"*Pīwakawaka*, I believe it is the Maori word for fantail." The chittering kept pace with us, but I couldn't see where the bird hid.

Frank chuckled and shook his head. "You, speaking Maori? Pull the other one, Gracie. You're just making it up."

The memory from when I touched Detective Archer echoed through my mind. The old woman's voice had been warm and lyrical. I wasn't making it up. But how to explain to Frank that a vision had taught me how to pronounce the word? "I heard someone say it. I think fantail sounds much nicer in Maori."

A scowl drew Frank's eyebrows together. "Why would you bother yourself with that nonsense?"

"Nonsense?" My feet froze to the ground and from above our heads, the bird appeared and lectured Frank.

"Come on, Gracie. No one speaks Maori, and we're English, aren't we?" He raised an arm to shoo away the bird.

"How can I be English when I was born here, and

I've never been to England? I think of myself as a New Zealander. Shouldn't we have some knowledge of the native language of this country? It's a tongue that was spoken here long before Captain Cook waded ashore in search of a hot meal." I never thought of myself as being politically minded, but something had changed in the last few weeks. Ever since the odd vision came over me, I found myself more alert to the way the first settlers of New Zealand were treated by all around me. As though someone had raised the blinds on a room in my mind, gestured to the land beyond, and told me to open my eyes and *look*.

Frank laughed even louder at my statement. "You're forgetting your history. We're British. Our ancestors brought civilisation to this country, and we fought to keep our way of life. Honestly, what's got into you, old girl?"

If there was one thing I detested, it was being called *old girl*. While meant as a term of endearment, it was what a farmer called his best sheepdog, who was expected to get back into line. A resolve was sprouting inside me to step *out* of line and march off down my own path.

But what had gotten into me? Perhaps, like that old reliable sheepdog, a flea had jumped into my fur and was agitating me to action. Except I didn't quite know what I could do, or even if I should do anything. Was it even appropriate for me to learn about the Maori when it wasn't my culture? I only knew I needed to scratch at the itch and see what happened.

"I've been thinking about all sorts of things lately." I shrugged it off.

Frank might not be open to the possibility of learning about other ways, but the idea stirred in me an excitement that mimicked the fantail's twittering.

Chapter Twelve

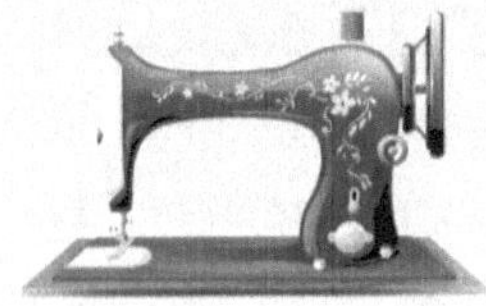

THAT NIGHT AFTER DINNER, I took a book and sat in the lounge, keeping one eye on the road beyond our cottage. Words swam on the page and my brain wouldn't co-operate. Then, as the light dimmed, the rumble of the motorcycle sounded. Joseph would need time to put the Triumph away in the shed and change out of his police uniform. While the clock ticked on the mantel, I closed the book and considered how to broach Mrs Taylor's memory, her son's displeasure at her expenditure, and the note I discovered.

"You look a thousand miles away, love," Dad said as I wandered back into the kitchen.

"I need to talk to Joseph about something." The longer letter could wait for another day. The threat to Ricky couldn't.

The time had come to be brave and have a quiet word with my cousin on a rather awkward topic. "I heard his motorcycle a little while ago, so I'm popping out to see him. I won't be long." I grabbed my coat from the hook by the back door.

"All right, love." Dad returned to his detective novel.

Hurrying up the street, I rapped on the door of where Joseph boarded with an elderly widow.

Mrs Cox answered the door. Her grey hair pulled back in a tight bun at her nape. The wrinkles in her face smoothed out as she smiled at seeing me. "Hello, Grace. If you're looking for Joseph, he hasn't come in for dinner yet. He changed out of his uniform and then went back out to the shed with that awful motor of his."

"Thank you, Mrs Cox. I'll go around the side. Have a lovely evening." I waved and then headed along the covered alleyway sandwiched in between two cottages.

I found Joseph in the shed at the rear of the property, doing something with an oil can, his screwdriver, and the now-silent motorcycle.

"Hello, Grace." While his greeting was warm, a wariness resided in his eyes.

My heart squeezed tighter for him. As a youth, he had been quick to smile and considerate of others. We all thought he would grow into a heartbreaker. Instead, war had broken him. What would it take for someone to sneak under the armour he now wore and heal his heart? Someone who could show him there was still joy and kindness in the world, while giving him a kick in the trousers when he deserved. Someone smart and loyal...like Etty. I tucked the idea away inside me.

While I was determined to see my cousin whole again, I had a murderer to find first.

"Hello, Joseph. Theo has a hamster now, and he named it Triumph, after your motorcycle." I leaned on the doorjamb, not wanting to venture in and dirty my shoes.

My comment elicited a quiet huff of laughter. "I bet you he ends up with one of his own when he's older."

I hoped not. The bone-jarring contraptions were death traps in my opinion. Silence fell in the shed and my gaze wandered the neatly stacked shelves and collection of tools hanging from nails.

"Not that I don't appreciate your company, but I don't think you sought me out to discuss motorcycles," he spoke with a quiet tone after several minutes.

"No. It's about Richard Hammond. I might know something, but it's information I learned in a *confidential* setting, and I'm not sure how to proceed." My cousin didn't know of my gift, and I needed a way to hint at what I saw without revealing I experienced it by touching Mrs Taylor.

He glanced up over the leather padded seat of the Triumph. "You mean like a priest's confessional?"

"Yes. Or the seamstress equivalent—the fitting room. I don't want to lose a client, Joseph, but I can't keep quiet if what I know is important to the investigation." What to do, ate at me. Obviously, I wanted to do the right thing, but sharing an intimate moment plucked from a woman's memory seemed so...wrong.

Like a thief creeping through a window of a darkened home and stealing a treasure from under your pillow.

"What makes you think it's important?" He placed the can of oil and screwdriver on a shelf and picked up a rag. With care, he wiped any oil and dirt from his fingers.

"I have a client who may have been *associated* with Ricky. Her son came into my shop and seemed rather upset at her wasting money on frivolous things." Little puzzle pieces slotted together like the torn strips of paper. On their own, they didn't seem like much. You had to lay them side by side and look at the entire thing to understand what they meant.

Joseph stared at me, a slight frown wrinkling his forehead. "That all sounds like a bit of a stretch."

"Yes. I know. But the thing is...there's this note, you see. It says 'Stay away from my mother, or else'. And I happen to know this client's son was at Days Bay that Saturday and in a rather angry mood after a waiter spilled his wine." I clasped my hands together and silently begged Mrs Taylor for her forgiveness.

"You have a note? Where did you get that?" He rose to his full height and nearly brushed against the corrugated iron roof of the shed.

"It was in the bottom of the hamster cage. I...we... that is Sam and I...we took the hamster from Ricky's bedroom last week. After the funeral. His flatmate was going to let it go in the bush." I cringed when Joseph's eyes widened. Would we be in trouble for making sure the little creature had clean water and a carrot to munch?

"Where is this note now?" His voice became clipped, as though he followed a police checklist in his head.

"I have it at home, of course. I've been waiting for a chance to talk to you about it." Pinned to its board, the note was too big to shove in a pocket and I didn't realise my chat with my constable cousin was supposed to include a show-and-tell segment.

He ground his jaw. "You need to talk to Detective Archer."

That was the bit that bothered me. Part of me wanted to pout and say no. There was something about the detective that rattled me as much as seeing the telegraph delivery man appear on our street. During the war, we would all hold our breath when the telegraph man strode along the road, wondering who would receive news that their soldier didn't make it. "Couldn't you do it for me? Please?"

The muscles in his face relaxed, and so did his tone. "He doesn't bite, Grace. I'll tell him tomorrow."

"Thank you, Joseph." I had a temporary reprieve, while I wracked my brain about what to tell Detective Archer. I could say it was a whispered confession, but all he had to do was ask Mrs Taylor and my fib would soon be hauled into the harsh daylight. How to word that I knew of a liaison between the older woman and Ricky without saying she told me?

Wednesday afternoon, I stood at the cutting table as a shadow passed by the window and, somehow, slipped into my shop without setting off the delicate tinkle of the bell over the top. My heart missed a beat as I recognised my adversary.

"Detective Archer," I muttered, grateful the expanse of the cutting table stood between us.

"Mrs Devine." He slid the fedora from his head.

Today he wore a suit of charcoal grey pinstripe. The cloth fitting his broad shoulders perfectly and I pondered if a detective earned enough to afford custom-made suits. Although probably a necessary expense for him. Anything off the rack would have been terribly uncomfortable every time he moved his arms. The crispness of his shirt was highlighted by a royal blue tie, and the same splash came from the handkerchief in the top pocket. The fashion critic in me approved of his appearance. So why did nerves ripple over my skin whenever he was near?

He placed the fedora on a corner of the table. "I'm here to discuss the Richard Hammond investigation."

My hand tightened on the tailor's shears in my hand. There was something about the man that made every guilty thought and action I ever had want to bubble to the surface. I had an overwhelming impulse to confess that since we had run late this morning, I had failed to make my bed.

"Those are rather lethal-looking scissors." He gestured to the item in my grip.

Oh, honestly! He couldn't possibly be suggesting what I think he was suggesting. "You can't seriously think I had anything to do with Ricky's death?" Before he could bamboozle me with his questions, I ploughed on. "Do you think I stabbed him with my scissors? These are important tools for my work, not beach toys. I don't let anyone else touch them, let alone take them from my shop for a jaunt to the seaside."

He opened his mouth, but in this, I refused to give any quarter. If he was going to arrest me, I was saying my piece first! "If I was going to stab someone in the back, I wouldn't use tailor's shears. I'd used dressmaker's scissors that have a much sharper point for cutting notches and ramming through someone's muscle!" To emphasise my comment, I picked up the shorter and lighter shears with my free hand and waved them in the air.

The ghost of a smile touched his lips and sparkled in his eyes. "I was merely commenting on the size of those scissors compared to the ones I use to snip string in my office."

Oh. A blush raced up from under my collar and bloomed across my cheeks. My brain had obviously gone to sleep and forgotten my conversation with Joseph only the previous night. He no doubt wanted to discuss the note. "I'm sorry for my outburst. You seem to have the capacity to make me feel guilty. It must be rather handy when interviewing suspects."

The smile twitched a smidge wider. "Constable Sullivan informed me that you removed the hamster from Mr Hammond's room and found something in its bedding."

Here was the bit where I hoped he wouldn't arrest me for tampering with evidence. Or was the neglected rodent a witness? "Yes. The poor thing looked quite bereft in its cage, and Mr Shadbolt wanted to let it go out into the bush. I took the animal home until Mr Hammond's family could be asked if they wanted it. My son is looking after Triumph. That's what he named the hamster. Triumph. After the motorcycle. Theo seems to be developing a distressing interest in anything fast and noisy." I babbled on as my brain raced ahead twenty years to the sort of speed-obsessed young man my child might become.

Detective Archer stepped closer and the faint aroma of sunlight soap and a sense of warmth danced around me and soothed my rattled nerves. "Thank you. When we searched Mr Hammond's room, I placed some food in the cage and changed the water. But couldn't do anymore at the time."

"I can return him to the police station if he is considered evidence or something. Although Theo and my father are already building a small race car for the hamster and that might have to accompany him. I'm not sure if hamsters regularly race automobiles, but apparently, this one now does." I put the shears down and picked up a pattern piece to keep my hands occupied.

The detective's shoulders heaved in silent laughter, and I swear he swallowed a smile. His eyes shone even as he tried to keep a serious look on his face. "I have been in touch with Mr Hammond's family and none of them want the hamster, so your son may keep him if he wants. I would hate to cut Triumph's racing career short."

A smile spread over my lips of its own accord at his words. Perhaps he wasn't so bad after all, as I glimpsed the kind soul lurking under the policeman's exterior. "Thank you. I shall let Theo know that Triumph can become a permanent part of the family."

"I am curious, though, as to what you found in the creature's bedding?" He unbuttoned his jacket, and my eyes were drawn to his fingers for a moment.

What were we discussing? Oh! The note. "Yes. When we cleaned out its cage, I noticed that Mr Hammond had used torn-up letters to line it. A word caught my attention, and, well...I admit in a fit of curiosity, I decided to see if I could put the note back together." Last night, I replaced the long pins with flat thumbtacks to keep the note in place, not wanting to use glue that couldn't be removed. Then I wrapped it in brown paper, to ensure nothing blew away on the walk to work.

Now, I fetched the parcel from where it sat beneath the counter and peeled off the wrapping. Then I handed it to the detective. An action akin to handing in your homework to the teacher at school and waiting to be graded.

He glanced at the note and nothing flickered across his face. No hint of whether I had done something of value or not. I was hoping for a pass grade on my project.

"My mother," he murmured. "Do you know who that refers to?" Now those dark eyes pinned me like a scrap of hamster-chewed paper.

"Yes. I believe so." I licked my lips. No lies would cross my tongue and I stuck to the truth. "Mrs Lynette Taylor. She and her son, Karl, had lunch at the Pavilion the day Mr Hammond died."

His attention on me never wavered. "And you believe there was some form of relationship between Mrs Taylor and Mr Hammond?"

In my mind's eye, Ricky stalked across an expensive rug towards a scantily clad Mrs Taylor who reclined on a bed. The image caused heat to race over my skin. Before I could find a way to answer the question, Detective Archer raised one eyebrow.

"I'll not ask you how you know. My enquiries had revealed that Mr Hammond was having a relationship with an older woman, but his associates didn't know who. I only needed a name, as he seemed to have kept that detail to himself." He rubbed the edge of the cardboard with his thumb.

A sigh of relief escaped me. "Thank you," I replied.

"Always a pleasure, Mrs Devine," he murmured. Then he placed the fedora back on his short ebony hair. With a nod, he left the shop as silently as he entered it.

Perplexed, I approached the door. Making sure he

had disappeared down Plimmer Steps, I pulled the door open. The bell gave its gentle tinkle. "How does he do that?" I wondered out loud.

"It's the way he opens the door. Smooth and gentle," Etty called out from her table. "I bet he's a fantastic dancer."

Chapter Thirteen

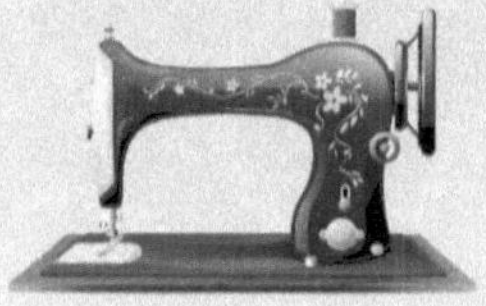

THURSDAY, Mrs Cooper arrived at my shop to review some sketches for her winter wardrobe. Once we had that part of our business concluded, we adjourned next door to the tiled entrance to the upstairs. My mentor took the small elevator while I trotted up the stairs to await her at the top.

The brass door drew back, and she stepped out. I clasped my hands together, waiting for her first impressions. Dad had created a reception area with a curved desk, currently hidden under a sheet to protect it while work continued. Mrs Cooper lifted one corner and peered underneath at the polished wood. "Oh, that is lovely work, and the shape is very modern."

While hiring a receptionist was a long way off, it made sense to construct the physical requirements of the business I imagined in my head. I gestured to the doors visible along the short and wide hall. "The fitting rooms are complete. I only need to source furnishings for them."

One side of the building held the reception, kitchenette, bathroom and storeroom. On the other side, we had transformed four former bedrooms into fitting rooms. The new silver and cream geometric wallpaper was, in my opinion, the perfect choice. Dad had replaced the plain glass in the windows with etched glass that let in the light, but no one could peer in from the opposite building. Dad was making me round platforms, where a client would stand before the mirrors while I adjusted a hem. I envisioned plush, velvet upholstered chairs in the corner, but they would need to wait until either Dad had time to make the frames, or I could find old ones we could reupholster. A sideboard would hold a vase of fresh flowers and gently scent the room.

"Elegant yet with a modern twist. It is looking fabulous, Grace." Mrs Cooper peered at the wall, inspecting the seam between the sheets of wallpaper.

"I was thinking a deep, moss green velvet for the chairs and sofas. I have some swatches we can look at before I decide on a fabric. Then there will be full-length mirrors on two walls, of course." Or there would be once I paid for them. I made excuses for the sparse rooms as though they were a child being criticised for a performance.

The old dame waved a hand. "You have the bones here, Grace, the rest is accessories. It is quite exciting to watch my fledgling grow stronger wings and ride higher currents. Just you wait, my dear, you are going to soar soon."

A blush heated my neck and face. At times, I had to pinch myself that Mrs Cooper believed in me. Dad was unwavering in his support, but...he was my father. He still kept a crayon scrawl I drew as a two-year-old because in his paternal delusion, he thought it was as good as any Monet.

"I have advertised for a new girl to help with the sewing and may possibly take on two if I have suitable candidates. As the business grows, I'll hire a shop girl for the ready-to-wear range downstairs, and eventually someone to sit at the front desk and take care of all the administration." So many staff, who would all be looking to me to generate enough work to pay every-one's wages. What if women stopped wanting gowns designed with Grace?

Imagining a dire future was a bomb lobbed into the middle of my dream. Bits of wallpaper burned as they drifted to the ground like fiery feathers. Spots danced before my eyes and red circled my vision. I placed a hand on my chest and drew a deep breath.

Mrs Cooper chuckled. "Just breathe, dear girl. You are only experiencing a little vertigo before you leap. But you are a sensible creature and you will not take on more than you can handle."

I nodded and my heart rate settled as I reminded myself that Dad and I had everything in hand. "Would you like to see the workroom?"

The wide hallway opened to the space occupying one end of the building. The tall windows and a skylight flooded it with light. One corner was closed off to create my office. Within, an angled desk sat under a window that perfectly illuminated my work. My own little domain where I could sketch and draw what would come to life in the main room.

In the middle of the floor stood a table so large, Dad had cut it into five pieces so that he and Joseph could get it up the stairs and into the space. Then the parts were assembled like giant jigsaw pieces. Dad had dove-tailed the edges so they would join together seamlessly. The very middle was a circle, the central point that made the pieces one magnificent cutting table.

"My...your father is quite the craftsman." Mrs Cooper walked around the substantial table, large enough to throw a bolt of fabric across. "Does he ever make smaller items of furniture?"

"Oh, yes. For my twenty-first, he made me a little Davenport to fit in my room with gorgeous art nouveau blooms up the legs. It even has secret drawers and, in my opinion, is as lovely as anything by Chippendale." I could never have raised the finances to expand my business without Dad's unfailing support and talent with wood. I had an artisan workspace that made my heart sing, but it cost us very little. Dad had a shed full of timber that he had collected over the decades and he gleefully dipped into it for the necessary raw materials. Then he added sweat and toil to make the pieces with Joseph's help when my cousin had spare time. Sam and I tackled the painting and wallpapering.

Around the room were four smaller tables where each seamstress would work. I imagined dress forms draped in vibrant colours against the soft cream walls. Another wall would soon be where the trusty Singer would sit and, in time, another would join it. Due to the floor's former life as rented lodgings, we even had a modest kitchen complete with hot and cold running water and a stove and a bathroom large enough to cope with the number of women who would eventually occupy the floor.

"If your father is up to a challenge, I would quite like a new drinks cabinet. One in the art deco style like the French are producing now, with soft curves and geometric lines. Ask him to draw some sketches, and I will commission a piece." Mrs Cooper strode towards the window and looked down on the narrow lane below.

"Thank you, Mrs Cooper. Do you have time to look at fabric samples for the upholstery?" I picked up the book of upholstery samples from its place on a smaller worktable and carried it to the larger one.

She turned and smiled. "Yes. Let us discuss the final touches. You will of course have a grand opening. With cocktails and a special showing for the upper echelon of Wellington society."

My brain stuttered. Special showings were something they did in Paris at grand fashion houses. Not in my little corner of the world in a building that used to be a boarding house. "I hadn't thought to do one. What if no one came?"

Mrs Cooper scoffed. "I shall arrange the invitations and the catering. You only need a few eye-popping pieces to make my friends reach deep into their purses."

For one night, we could turn the workroom into a theatrical space before we knuckled down. All I needed was a few jaw-dropping gowns. And the time to design and create them. "The idea is marvellous if I can manage it. We are rather busy with the dresses women want to wear to events over the course of the royal visit." A few of my clients were even journeying to Auckland to meet the prince at functions up there. They probably hoped to catch his eye before he made it to Wellington and have an engagement ring before his ship departed once more for England.

I opened the heavy book of swatches and slid my hands in at the start of the green samples and levered the reds and blues to one side. As we discussed each shade, pattern, and type of fabric, I struggled with a way to turn the conversation to the topic my curiosity wanted to discuss. I was aware the two women knew each other, as Mrs Cooper had accompanied Mrs Taylor on her first visit to my little shop some four years ago.

As we neared the end of the samples, I decided to just spill out my question. "Do you know Mrs Lynette Taylor, well?"

"Oh, yes. Lynette is entertaining company. Especially after she's had a few gins. That earned her a place within my small circle of friends. I was rather glad when she found someone to put the sparkle back in her eye these last few months. But the young buck seems to have romped off to greener pastures and left her in a glum mood." Mrs Cooper rubbed a thumb over the thick pile of a velvet before flipping to the swatch of a brocade.

"He didn't leave her." The words tumbled from me before I could recall them.

A sharp blue gaze regarded me. "You know who he is. Do tell, so I might chastise him for hurting my friend."

Words bubbled up, but I put a cork on them as I struggled with the dilemma of sharing the scandalous details. Part of me wanted to blurt out that the much younger Ricky had put the sparkle into Mrs Taylor's eyes. But another part of me held tight to the intimate details of the private life of my client. My conscience whispered it was wrong to snatch a memory without the other person's knowledge or consent and to then share it with others.

Mrs Cooper turned from the book and placed a hand on my arm. "You are loyal and don't want to break a confidence. I admire that, Grace. Lynette is a close friend of mine and if you are concerned about spreading gossip, I can assure you that you are not. I am aware my friend found a younger man to lavish atten-tion on her and that would earn her censure from some.

But never from me. Happiness is too precious a thing, to cast scorn on someone else for where they find it."

I swallowed and washed away some of the resistance in my throat. "I don't believe he intended to leave her. It was just that he died. Or rather, was murdered."

"Murdered?" Mrs Cooper's eyes widened, and she looked away as I suspect she scanned her memory of recent events. "That smiling chap who has been in the newspaper. Died swimming, if I remember correctly?"

Wellington wasn't exactly known for its murder rate. They happened seldom and there was only one that had dominated talk for some weeks. "Yes," I whispered. "Richard Hammond. He was stabbed."

A sigh blew from my mentor and ruffled the feathered brooch on her jacket. "Poor Lynette. She has had rotten luck in love recently."

That piqued my interest. Had Mrs Taylor lost more than one lover? "Oh? Has another *special friend* of hers met an unexpected end?"

"Why do you ask?" Mrs Cooper returned to the samples and flipped through the hard-wearing cottons.

I made a decision to include the grand dame in the circle of confidentiality I erected around all my clients. As both a client and a friend of Mrs Taylor, she would have the best interests of the other woman at heart. "The other day, Mrs Taylor's son came in here and his...words and actions aroused my curiosity. He seemed rather incensed at what he called her frivolous expenditure."

Mrs Cooper huffed. "Karl. He's a spoiled brat, that one. She should have sent him off to war to put some lead in his spine. Certainly wouldn't hurt him to toil for a full day to earn his pay, instead of whining and clinging to his mother's purse."

To that list, I would add that he could stop referring to his mother as *Mummy*. Putting aside my distaste for that, there was a larger matter that concerned me. "Mr Taylor tapped the newspaper article about Richard Hammond's death when he made mention of curbing her spending in one area. It seemed so odd that I can't help but wonder..."

"You think Karl might have done a little judicious pruning of his mother's spending?" Mrs Cooper worded my suspicion.

"You said that Mrs Taylor has been unlucky in love. Do you think her son doesn't like anyone else getting too close to his mother?" Angry words scrawled on a note floated before me...STAY AWAY from my mother.

"Oh, I don't think it. I know it. He doesn't want another chap potentially replacing his departed father and the associated risk that his mother might change her will in favour of a new husband." Mrs Cooper turned back to a particular sample of velvet.

"Gosh." Some days, Sam and I would dream of all we would do if we were wealthy. But money came with its own problems. Imagine family and friends only liking you because of what you have, rather than who you are. "What happened to the other gentleman?"

"That I do not know. Everything seemed to be going well between them. Certainly, Lynette never mentioned any problems. The chap simply dropped out of her life one day. But I always wondered if Karl had scared him off. I've not seen him since." She held up two very similar greens and angled them towards the light.

Could Karl have done more than scare the previous romantic interest away? How ghastly for his mother to never be allowed to love again. "Do you remember his name?"

Having selected her choice of upholstery fabric, Mrs Cooper turned and leaned against the cutting table. "Russell Norton. An older gentleman. A bit dull, I thought, but Lynette enjoyed his company."

I tucked the name away for later. Then another thought occurred to me. "You don't think Mrs Taylor is in any danger, do you?" Why chase off a procession of men when he could push his mother down the stairs and claim the lot?

"It wouldn't do him much good. His father was a shrewd judge of character and tied up Karl's inheritance in a trust until he turns thirty-five. Even if Lynette were to expire, and I certainly hope she lives many more years, her estate will be added to the same trust. Karl will simply have to bide his time until then." With a fingertip, Mrs Cooper traced one of the dovetail joins that gave the tabletop a unique look.

As I escorted Mrs Cooper back to the elevator, I

wondered why Karl Taylor couldn't be satisfied with what he had. His family's money allowed him a lifestyle few of us could imagine, and yet he sought more. Then I thought of my family, and Sam's. We were working class and appreciated every penny we earned. Yet our lives were full of love and we had enough.

Chapter Fourteen

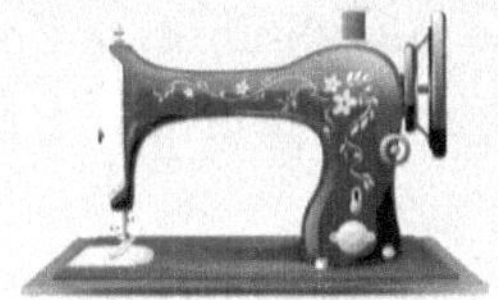

THAT AFTERNOON AFTER WORK, I joined Sam out in our shared backyard. There was still a little warmth in the sun, even though we moved into autumn and the trees protected us from the wind shaking the tops of the boughs.

"I spoke to Detective Archer today and gave him the note." I sank into the deckchair next to my friend.

Sam stared at the clouds forming above. "That should be enough to get them to drop Harry as a suspect and go arrest this rich chap."

"I saw Frank on Monday. He said Ricky associated with a bit of a rough crowd at a pub called the Scrum and Tackle." After learning that, Frank and I had come close to an argument. All over my use of one Maori word and my desire to learn more about a culture that had been almost hidden from the view of most New Zealanders.

"I've heard of the place. It's popular with the

labouring lads who come into the bakery. Can't see how it would be relevant, though, when we've got a bloke writing threatening letters to Ricky." Sam pulled apart a daisy and tossed the petals to the light breeze.

"There's more. Apparently, Mrs Taylor had another beau who just disappeared one day, and she never saw him again," I whispered the words as my brain whirled.

Sam let out a whistle. "You think her son is offing anyone who might get their hands on her money?"

I was fairly certain Ricky had laid his hands on more than Mrs Taylor's money. But had he genuinely liked the lonely woman, or had it all been an act to elevate his lifestyle? And why did he pretend to like Harry? I still couldn't fit that piece into the puzzle that was Richard Hammond. "Possibly Karl Taylor might have done it before. And got away with it."

"And if he got away with it once, he might get away with it again," Sam's words echoed my thoughts.

A worried tinge in Sam's words caught my attention. "Do you still think the police might arrest Harry?"

"He's an easy target. Not like a rich man with influence. There was another attack last night and still the cops do nothing." She brushed daisy petals from her hands and leaned back against her chair.

A sad breath escaped my lungs. "Who was it?"

"A nice gent. Not in my direct circle, but I knew him enough to smile and wave. I heard about it this morning. He's an accountant, and they stomped on his hand and broke his fingers." Her hands curled into fists.

Perhaps imagining how her life would be ruined if she lost the use of her hands.

I clasped mine together, to reassure my fingers that they could still caress fabric and stitch an invisible hem. Leaning back in the deckchair I closed my eyes, as I tried to figure out how to solve the problems plaguing my friends. Someone was targeting members of their close-knit community, and it bothered me that law enforcement wouldn't protect them. Were prejudices so deeply ingrained in our society, that they could condone such horrid actions? "Someone needs to tell the police about the motives behind the attacks. It can't be allowed to go on. Someone will get killed."

Sam let out a snort. "Our stupid laws say that what some men do is illegal. Who wants to report that as the reason for the beatings? These lads would rather go home to recover from their wounds than end up facing far worse in prison."

The familiar indignation surged through my torso. It shouldn't be like that. How could two men end up in prison for liking each other, when the thug who beat them up got to walk away without any punishment? "Something needs to change. Perhaps I should ask Arthur Shadbolt how you go about getting laws over-turned and start a petition or something."

"Even if we achieved that and changed the laws, you can't cure stupid. Some people will always want to tear apart what they don't understand or what frightens them." Sam spoke in a soft, resigned tone.

I reached out and took her hand. "You are my best

friend in this world, and I love you for who you are. I might not be able to change the world, but I can raise a child free of such prejudices. Every day, I promise I will do whatever I can to dismantle such beliefs when I encounter them."

"My mum always says you don't need a lot of friends, just a few good ones. You're a good one, Grace." She rose from her chair and knelt by mine to wrap her strong arms around me.

Tears moistened my eyes. Sam was, quite simply, the best friend in the entire world. By my side, through thick and thin. She even let me dig my nails into her palms when I had Theo, and she was the one who told me I could do it when I thought the stubborn child was never going to make his entrance into the world.

Thinking of my son reminded me of an upcoming event. I let go of Sam, took hold of her shoulders, and looked her square in the eyes. "Sam, brace yourself... Theo wants a racing car birthday cake."

Her eyes widened briefly, then she burst out laughing. Sucking her lips together, she donned a serious expression. "I think I can make a racing car. What colour does he want?"

"Red. Apparently, red cars go faster, although I'm not sure how he knows since every motor around here is either black or very dark blue." I suspected Dad was reading out the articles about car races to Theo, and they always devoted several lines to describing each death trap.

Sam squeezed my hand. "I can manage a red car."

Biting my lip to stop the grin that wanted to escape, I leaned close and added, "With a hamster at the wheel."

We both dissolved into laughter, and my heart felt light and full at the same time. Why did love and companionship weigh so little that we could carry an abundance of it with ease? Then I thought of Mrs Taylor and her sulky son. We didn't need money when we had something more important—each other.

After dinner, I fetched another sheet of cardboard to start on the second letter. This one took longer with its long and cramped sentences. Thankfully, the scribe had a flourish to their penmanship and the swooping lines helped link the top and bottom rows. The hand-writing struck me as having the care and attention of a woman wielding the pen.

"I'm off to bed, love." Dad rose from his chair.

My gaze darted to the clock, the small hand reaching for the ten. Gosh, where had the time gone?

I angled my face for his goodnight kiss on the top of my head. "I'll not be much longer. I want to get this finished."

Dad huffed in laughter. "Never thought what you find in the bottom of a hamster cage would be so...absorbing."

I grinned at him. "I know it seems silly, but an itch

at the back of my head said there might be something important here."

Only three strips remained in the basket. Before long, I picked up the last sliver of paper and pinned it in place. Then I arched my back to relieve muscles as tight as when I had hunched over the Singer to finish Agatha's gown before her fatal party. Excitement bubbled up as I scanned the letter. Then I deflated. All that effort for the ramblings of what was probably Ricky's great aunt. She described the disappointment of her tomato crop this season. Then she said a niece called Victoria dreamed of attending university in Auckland. The lavender under her window had taken off and needed cutting back. The letter finished by detailing how she needed to go to the library and speak to the librarian about a book she couldn't find.

"Well, at least one note might be a clue," I muttered as I put everything away. There would be no point in handing this one over to the detective, but I would store it away in case they asked for it. Fetching a sheet of brown paper, I slid it under the cardboard and folded it across the top. The paper didn't quite reach the other side of the board and obscured most of the text on the right-hand side. The gap left the first word of each sentence picked out in a vertical row.

Don't
disappoint
again
Victoria
University

lavender

librarian

"Oh," exhaled from my lungs. Maybe it was my imagination, but that sounded a lot like a coded message about Harry. The librarian at Victoria University who preferred the company of men. Which meant the attacks were not only targeted, but Ricky had somehow been involved. *Don't disappoint again.*

"What were you involved in, Ricky?" I asked the row of words.

Not finding any answers in the slumbering cottage, I packed away the letter, turned off the lights, and crept up to my bedroom. Upstairs, I crawled into bed and lay on my back, staring at the slanted ceiling in the softness of night. My thoughts swirled with snatches of memory, images, and words. Some hate-fuelled group was attacking certain men. Ricky had entered a friendship with Harry that the latter thought had romantic overtones. But then Ricky had ended their fledgling relationship to continue his liaison with Mrs Taylor.

Had he genuinely liked Harry, or had it been a ruse to confirm the words my brain picked out in the letter? What if Harry had been the next intended target of the thugs? Another entirely plausible explanation was that my overactive imagination was seeing things that weren't there. Who knew? Perhaps most letters revealed a cryptic message when you read the first word from each line vertically. And yet...something itched at my brain. A clue that I overlooked and yet a compulsion drove me on, urging that once I found the missing piece, everything would make sense.

A tiny version of myself sat surrounded by hundreds of memories as it tried to figure out what I had overlooked. Leaving it up to my sub-conscious to do the work, I drifted off to sleep.

The next morning I dropped Theo off a bit earlier at Mrs Rogers's for the day and then headed for the Kostas bakery. I selected two delicious-smelling date scones for morning tea while I waited for Sam to have a spare moment.

"What is it?" As she came around the side of the counter, Sam wiped flour from her hands onto her apron.

I glanced around as a customer moved forwards to order with Mrs Kostas, then leaned closer to my friend. "I pieced together the other letter last night. Now this might not be anything, but it's chewing at me. I think it contained a coded message to Ricky to get close to Harry."

"Why..." Sam's eyes widened, and the syllable came out louder than she expected. Lowering her tone, she continued, "You think Ricky was setting up men for the gang of thugs to beat up?"

"I don't know. Who made the first contact between them—Harry or Ricky?" I desperately wanted to discount the wild theory. Even saying it out loud seemed silly.

Sam blew out a snort, and a strand of hair floated off her forehead. "I don't know. Harry often called in here to grab something for his lunch before heading up to the university." The door opened as more customers came into the bakery before work. "We need to talk to Harry. Can you finish a bit earlier?"

"Yes." I owed Etty some time off, and I could always catch up over the weekend.

"I'll collect you when I'm off here." Sam hurried back behind the counter.

I clutched the bag with the scones and waved goodbye to Sam and her mother as they served the hungry workers.

Etty and I had a busy day that didn't allow any time for thoughts of murder and roaming gangs of things. Then I sent my assistant home early. By the time Sam pushed the door open, I had tidied up and was ready to go. We collected Theo first and deposited him at home with Dad. That gave me a chance to change clothes.

We chatted as we headed along to the university.

"What are your plans for tomorrow night?" Sam asked, with a sparkle in her eyes.

"Most likely a good book and a cup of cocoa. But I have a feeling that is about to change." We crossed the road and headed along the Terrace. Frank's words echoed through my mind, that a woman of my age should be out enjoying life and not at home like a nana.

Perhaps I could branch out...and read more adventurous books?

Sam looped her arm through mine. "I have to deliver a load of pies to the Scrum and Tackle tomorrow. The All Blacks have a warm-up game ahead of the New South Wales tour, and the bar wants to feed their punters. Thought you might like to assist."

"Oh, yes. But I'll have to check with Dad that he's all right with Theo for a few hours." My father was an exceptional grandparent. He never grumbled about feeding Theo and putting him to bed, so I could have a few hours to myself. But I never took his help for granted. After Mum left, he devoted years to raising me and then rolled up his sleeves to start changing nappies again with Theo. I wondered why he never cast around for a companion for his later years, or if Mum had broken his heart and it never healed.

We cut through Kelburn Park to reach the red brick Hunter Building that contained the library.

My shoes seemed overly loud on the hardwood floors as we walked the aisle between stacks of books and the reading desks. A few students were bent over books. Some scribbled notes. One stared at the text with confusion written across his face. I recognised the dishevelled hair and dark-rimmed spectacles of Arthur Shadbolt among those writing copious notes.

We found Harry between two stacks, an armload of books in his embrace as he returned them to their proper location.

"Hello, you two. This is a surprise," he spoke softly

upon seeing us. He had removed his jacket but wore a russet-coloured waistcoat that made me think of autumn leaves. The tone complimented his dark cream business shirt. A deep red tie finished his stylish ensemble.

"Do you have time to talk?" Sam whispered.

Harry eased a book into a tight gap between two others. "If we're not too long. Can't trust that lot out there. Some of them try to write in the margins. Can you believe it?" He shook his head and tutted under his breath at the desecration of the books under his care.

"We shouldn't take up too much of your time," I murmured.

We followed Harry back along the aisle, where he deposited the books on the corner of his desk. With a warning glare at the students at the reading desks, we climbed the short, open stairwell and exited the building.

Out in the sun, we found a private spot in the shelter of the building and away from the students rushing to and from classes. "It's about Ricky, isn't it?"

"Yes. I know you used to see him in the bakery, but who made the first social advance between you?" I wanted to be wrong. I needed my imagination to have picked on random words and assigned them meaning. I didn't want ignorant men targeting others simply because of who they were inside their skin.

Harry huffed and fell silent for a long moment. "Ricky. From memory, I saw him here and asked if he was lost. He said he was taking a shortcut past the university and then he asked if I wanted to get a drink with him."

I glanced at Sam. Bother.

"Why is that important?" The librarian narrowed his gaze.

"I think you were targeted. Ricky was sent a note about the librarian at the university, and...there he was that day." My shoulders sagged, disappointed in the young man. Not that his actions meant he in any way deserved to have his life taken, but the police should have dealt with him and his associates.

"You think I was supposed to be the next victim of that bunch of *cowards*? But then why did he break up with me and say he had found someone else?" Harry crossed his arms and his fingers tightened into the cotton of his shirt.

He raised a valid question. One for which I couldn't supply an answer.

Chapter Fifteen

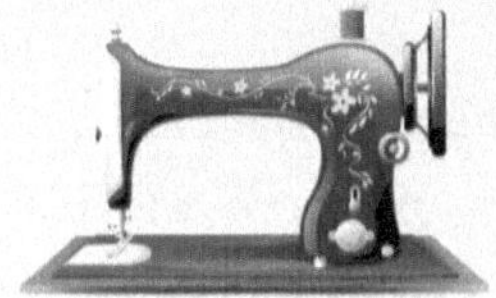

Over the rest of the day and into Saturday, Ricky's actions gnawed at the back of my mind, like a mouse nibbling the plaster in the middle of the night. Why hadn't he lured Harry out to some dark alley? Or had the former bakery employee had a change of heart?

Early Saturday evening, I dressed in wide-legged navy trousers and a pale cotton shirt before meeting Sam at the bakery. The two Kostas women had worked all day to make a hundred pies for the men. Twenty-five were stacked into each of four trays and then loaded onto the back of the cart. Sam and I climbed up beside the driver as the horse carried us the short distance to the club. Sound rippled from the small windows and drifted across the road, and I could only imagine how noisy it was inside.

The driver urged the horse down the alley and around the back. Rubbish cans lined one wall, against the other were wooden crates crammed with empty beer bottles, all waiting to be replaced with full ones by the brewery. A door was propped open with an old brick to let air into the building.

Sam jumped down and stuck her head in the open door, calling out. "Hello? Delivery from Kostas Bakery."

I waited by the cart, the aroma of all those freshly baked pies tickling my nose and making my stomach rumble. At home, Dad would be serving up the joint of mutton I had put in the oven earlier in the day for our dinner.

Sam reappeared and gestured with her head towards the door. "Mr Smithers, the owner, is run off his feet in there. The lads are thirsty with all the shouting. Let's carry the pies through for him."

Taking an end of a tray each, we manoeuvred the first one through the door. I found myself in a small kitchen with a square table dominating the middle of the space. We placed the tray on the table and then fetched the next one. Soon, we had all four trays stacked on the table.

At that point, a flustered-looking gentleman, somewhere in his fifties, rushed into the kitchen. He possessed the red, rotund face and barrel shape of a publican who liked to sample the brew. "Brilliant, Miss Kostas. The troops out there are hungry and starting to howl, and we've only just had kick-off." Mr Smithers looked at the trays with a slight air of despair.

"Do you need some extra hands? My friend and I

are happy to stay and help for a couple of bob each," Sam offered.

Relief washed over him. "I'll not say no to some extra hands. I only have my wife helping behind the bar, and we're going full-tilt just to keep up with pouring jugs." He opened a cupboard where platters were stacked in a tall pile. "Ten pies to a platter, one platter per table. Can I leave you to do that? I need to get pouring beers."

"Shouldn't you have closed the bar by now? It's after six-thirty." I glanced at my wristwatch, the minute hand hovering over the six. The pub was a good half-hour late in calling time.

He grinned and tapped the side of his nose. "No worries there, love. The coppers turn a blind eye when a match is being played. Besides, with giving that lot the pies, we can say we are a restaurant and allowed to be open until eight."

I glanced at Sam. My worries were not placated by his reassurances. In fact, they proliferated instead, pondering if a few pies were sufficient to meet the definition of a restaurant. Then my brain resolved the dilemma by pointing out *we* weren't breaking the rules about pubs not being allowed to serve alcohol after six, as we were simply delivery girls. With that internal conflict settled, for the moment, Sam and I set to work placing pies in two tiers on each platter.

"Ready?" Sam said as we both picked up a large plate each. The noise from beyond the door grew in intensity, and I gathered someone had made it across the line with the ball.

I nodded, and she pushed the door open with her backside, and we stepped into the main bar. Another roar went up at our appearance, or most likely that of food. The sound hit me like a physical thing, coming from all those bodies crammed into the small bar. I made for the closest table, glad I had chosen trousers. Men after a few beers could get handsy, and I didn't want any of them thinking they could touch my stockinged legs. Mr Smithers and his wife were engaged in a non-stop chain of pulling pints, taking them to tables, picking up empties, and starting all over again. Men listening to a rugby match on the wireless had a prodigious capacity to drink beer.

The radio blared the live relay of the game of our boys, known as the Invincibles or more commonly because of their black uniforms—the All Blacks. Cheers went up as one of our players surged across the field, promptly followed by a round of boos when the Aussies took control of the ball.

I deposited the platter on the table, as men called out their thanks and fell upon the pastry shells like seagulls fighting over chips. I scurried back for another platter. Winding my way through sweaty bodies, my imagination couldn't place smiling Ricky among this rough crowd. But I didn't doubt Frank's sources of information. I scanned the men, wondering who among them were the Bin Men and Geoff Dwyer.

As I pushed past two arguing gents to place the

next platter on a table, another thought crossed my mind...was Etty's brother here this evening? Could the old rugby player called Geoff, who led young Patrick into trouble, be the same Geoff who led the Bin Men? I had asked Joseph if he could take the troubled youth under his wing, but because of my cousin's shifts, we had yet to connect the two.

I kept my eyes open for the same auburn hair as Etty but couldn't do that, keep the platter level, and watch out for the rambunctious men. Delivering their meal seemed as fraught as making a run for the end of the field with the Roos swarming behind me, trying to tackle me off my feet.

We were down to the last two platters when someone yelled out, "Dwyer!"

A broad man at a table in the far corner swung his head.

I had found him.

The veteran's ears showed the characteristic bulbous swelling (the result of constant trauma from scrums) that earned them the name *cauliflower* ears. Mr Dwyer's nose had been broken at least once and either badly set or he had thumped it back into place himself, given the odd kink in it. While not overly tall, from what I could tell due to him being seated, he possessed a broad muscular build similar to that of Detective Archer. But the detective's bulk gave me the impression of someone who used his strength to defend. Geoff Dwyer projected an air of intimidation.

"What are you staring at, love?" His small, bleary eyes pinned me to the spot.

I struggled with what to say. "I'm so sorry. You look familiar, and I cannot place where I have seen you. It must be in the newspapers. Are you a famous rugby player?" I added a breathy hitch to my voice and played the part of the overwhelmed fan.

He grinned. "I was, once. I would have been one of the Invincibles but for the damn war."

"What happened?" I placed the platter in the middle of his table, and he picked up a pie with a beefy hand.

"Shrapnel. But I don't want to talk about that. What's a pretty thing like you doing in trousers? Pretending to be one of the boys, are you?" His top lip pulled back in a sneer as those around him laughed.

"I think trousers are practical when working. Besides, if a woman can be one of the boys, can't a boy be one of the girls?" I grabbed an empty jug, thinking I could return it to the bar to save Mrs Smithers the trip or use it to bash someone's head if they got too friendly.

"Men should be men, and women should be women," one of the men across the table said.

Noises of agreement rose from around the table.

Tightening my grip on the jug, I placed a smile on my lips. "I think people should be free to express who they are on the inside, and what they do in private is their own business and no one else's."

Geoff's hand shot out, and he grabbed my wrist. "Everyone has a place in this life, and they should stick to it. That's how we keep order. Someone needs to teach those dandy men a lesson in how to be real men."

I let out a gasp as a memory clawed its way from him into my brain.

The worm crawled on the ground at my feet. I kicked him, ignoring the pain from the shrapnel in my thigh. It was worth it.

'Piece of trash!'

They shouldn't pollute our streets, and we were going to clean them all out like the rubbish they were.

"What's wrong, little fellow? If you can't handle the grip of a strong man, take off the trousers, put a dress on like a good little woman, and get back to that kitchen." He pushed me, and I stumbled a step.

"It seems we have different views on the world, sir." And yours are abhorrent and small-minded, I wanted to shout. But I kept my retort inside my head, as I had enough common sense not to provoke a brawl in the middle of a rugby game while surrounded by beer-soaked lads.

After dropping the empty jug on the counter, I hurried back to the kitchen. My heart pounded from the ugliness of the memory shoved into my brain. I had found those behind the brutal attacks on some members of our community, and yesterday's events revealed the horrible role Ricky had played in their games. Bait.

Thankful that we had finished our task of serving the pies, I stuck my head back through the door to find

Sam. As I spotted my friend returning from the last table, a shrill whistle sounded.

Full time already? Then I realised the noise hadn't come from the radio but from the front door.

"Coppers!" a man yelled, as men in dark blue uniforms, truncheons drawn, flowed in through the door.

Arguments erupted (probably about the nuanced difference between a pub and a restaurant) and I grabbed Sam's hand and pulled her back into the kitchen. We turned to find our path blocked by the tall bulk of Joseph and two other officers, who must have entered through the back door.

My cousin's hands clasped around my upper arms and his eyes crinkled with concern. "Grace. What on earth are you doing here?"

"Sam and I delivered a load of pies," I stammered. I'd never been in a raid before, and my wild imagination clothed me in prison grey for simply lending a helping hand.

He let out a sigh. "You ladies are in trouble for working in a bar that's served beer after closing time. You're going to have to wait outside." He gestured for us to go stand in the rear courtyard.

"The owner said it was all above board because he was serving food," I stammered as Joseph cast me a disappointed look.

Like naughty children sent to report to the headmaster, Sam and I stood out in the yard. A bored policeman kept watch. More whistles sounded from inside the bar, the crack of wood splitting, and shouted cries. A glance at my watch told me it was seven-thirty, and I hazarded a guess Mr Smithers had failed to convince the police the pub became a restaurant after the addition of a hundred pies.

The light dulled as twilight edged into night, and the raucous noise dropped away. A familiar shape was silhouetted in the doorway, light spilling over his broad shoulders. Despite the brawl, his suit jacket was still done up and his fedora was straight on his head.

"Mrs Devine. Miss Kostas. I did not expect to see your names as working here." Detective Archer approached us.

"We don't. The owner ordered a large number of pies from my bakery to feed his punters while they listened to the game." Sam spoke up as my vocal cords always struggled to operate around the detective and his piercing stare.

I edged closer to my friend in the growing dark and laced our fingers together.

"Mr Smithers said you are both in his pay." Detective Archer stopped an arm's length from us.

"He and his wife were ever so busy, so we offered to plate up the pies and take them out to the tables," I said, drawing strength from Sam's presence at my side.

"You received payment, though. Which would make you employees." His questions were quiet on the still air. An eerie calm descended now that all the patrons had been cleared out of the little pub.

Words dried up on my tongue, but thankfully Sam

was more quick-witted. Or less susceptible to whatever power the senior policeman seemed to wield over my senses.

"You're wrong. He never paid us," Sam said. "Can we be on our way, now? We both need to get home to our families."

"In a moment. I have one more question." Detective Archer regarded me with unfathomably dark eyes, like staring at a starless sky trying to comprehend the size of the universe. "You do not draw a war widow's pension, Mrs Devine, and I wondered why not."

My brain froze, and my eyes widened. Breath came a little shorter in my chest and by squeezing my palms together, I slowed my breathing before I hyperventilated. "Pardon?" Was all I could muster up.

"During our previous...association...I closely examined your background while seeking out who killed Miss Agatha Marshall. I found it odd that you don't draw the war widow's pension. It is something of a loose end from that investigation." He dropped his gaze and straightened the cuffs of his shirt so they both jutted out the exact same one inch from his jacket sleeve.

Before answering, I swallowed. "I make sufficient from my own endeavours to support my family. I'll not be a burden upon this government."

"Mr Devine died while serving his country, leaving you to raise your son alone and you are entitled to those funds." He tilted his head and a quizzical expression flashed across his face. As though I was a puzzle he couldn't solve.

"If you dug so deeply into my background," and good lord, I hoped he hadn't dug too deep, "then you know that Freddie and I were only married for a few days before he shipped out. It never sat right with me to draw a widow's pension when we never experienced married life." Try as I might, I didn't regret that. I suspected we would have had an unhappy marriage as Freddie chased other women, and I was treated like a charlady.

One groomed eyebrow arched. "Actually, I couldn't find the exact date of your marriage. Or any record of it."

The blood in my veins chilled. "I fail to see how the intimate aspects of my private life have any relevance to a bar breaching six o'clock closing. That aside, do you know how many couples rushed to marry before our soldiers shipped out?"

Something dark passed behind his eyes and his fingers flexed around the bottom button on his jacket. Had I touched a memory there?

"I cannot be held responsible if the details were incorrectly written down. There were so many of us. The ceremonies were done with at least half a dozen couples crammed into the room at a time. All of us wanting to seal our love before war tore you away." Finding a rare vein of bravery, I boldly met his stare as I said my piece. Pain flared in his eyes before he looked away. Ah. I had touched a nerve. Had no one loved him enough to want to marry him in haste?

"As you said, the details are not relevant to this investigation. I shall let you both go with a warning." He touched the brim of his hat and retreated into the dark.

Chapter Sixteen

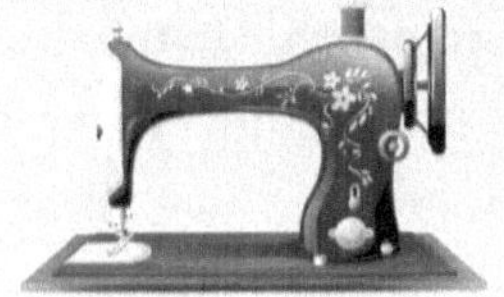

SAM and I were quiet on the walk home. Too many images and thoughts were crammed into my head, and I struggled to pull one out to discuss. If I tugged on one, I suspected the whole lot would tumble out in an utter mess. Rather like flinging open the door on an over-stuffed cupboard.

"Now that we have seen the sort that Ricky associated with, we need to talk about what to do now," I said as we approached our street.

Sam's grip tightened on my hand. "I wonder if we're best to leave it to the police. They're a rough lot, Grace. I heard what he said to you just for wearing a pair of trousers. You could have got hurt, and I'm sorry I dragged you into this."

I stopped not far from our cottages and, letting go of her hands, turned to face her. "I know why they call themselves the Bin Men. It has nothing to do with being sent off the field. They see themselves as clearing the rubbish off the streets. That's what they think of people like Ricky...and you...rubbish." The words tasted foul on my tongue, but she needed to know the full extent of Ricky's involvement with the group.

Sam's hands tightened into fists and her jaw clenched, but she remained silent.

I wrapped my hands over her closed ones and shook them gently. "People are getting hurt. Even if we can't find who killed Ricky, maybe we can at least stop that gang of thugs he was tied up with."

She shook her head, then tugged me towards the soft lights of home. "You were right, we're not police or investigators. We're just a baker and a seamstress. We should leave it to Joseph and the rest of the boys in blue."

I'd never seen my friend look so deflated, and my heart ached. "I will *never* stand by while injustices happen and say it's not my problem, or I shouldn't get involved. It's when seamstresses, and bakers, and carpenters get involved that we can make changes in the world. Did women get the vote by waiting around for men to give it to us?"

Her lips quirked in a smile. "No. Our mothers, aunties, and grandmothers fought for change."

"This is the same. You have rights and we must make a stand for them." Never in my wildest dreams did I cast myself as a revolutionary. I was merely a working mum who wanted a kinder world for those she loved.

Sam drew herself up and shook off whatever

pressed on her mind. "But what happened to Ricky doesn't fit with how this gang operates. He was stabbed in the back, not beaten. Maybe we should find out more about Karl Taylor and his mother's other companion who disappeared?"

"Maybe you're right," I murmured as we reached my gate. When Geoff Dwyer had grabbed hold of me, the look in his eyes had made a slice of fear slide down between my shoulder blades. But he struck me as a man who liked to use his fists. A knife in the back seemed more cowardly—like a rich, spoiled man would do. "I'll talk to Mrs Cooper, see if I can learn anything more."

We said our goodnights and parted company.

In the warm space that combined our kitchen and dining room, Dad sat in his favourite chair with his legs up on a stool and a book in his lap. He looked up as I walked in. "You're late, love. Did you stay to listen to the game?"

I pulled out a dining room chair, dropped to the seat, and toed off my Oxfords, so I could wriggle my toes. "No. The pub got raided for breaking six o'clock closing. I suspect Joseph will have a word to you about my presence there."

Dad put his book down and huffed. "He's just looking out for you like a brother would."

"I know. Honestly, he didn't have to say a word. He had such a look of disappointment in his eyes you would think I had scratched his motorcycle." I loved my cousin and Dad was right. He was close enough that he acted like a brother. Which meant he annoyed me like only a brother could, too. I worried about him in return and wanted him to find happiness in life.

"The owner was an idiot if he kept serving pints after six. The Arms closes the bar, but lets the lads gather around the wireless." Dad rose and hobbled over to the kitchen. He pulled a plate from the warming drawer and set it on the table for me.

In stocking-clad feet, I padded around to make myself a cup of cocoa to go with my dinner. "The owner thought serving pies made the Scrum and Tackle a restaurant. It seems the local constabulary disagreed."

"They might have looked the other way if that place didn't have such a reputation for trouble. I'm glad you're home unscathed. Theo insisted on a story about race cars tonight. I'm worried about that child. He might grow up waiting to join the army instead of the navy like his poppa. I need to find him more books with sea adventures and pirates." He took a seat opposite me at the table.

"Don't worry, I have a bumper book of sea stories on order with the bookstore. It should arrive in time for his birthday."

As March edged closer to April, Theo became more excited about his upcoming birthday and finally being a big boy who went to school. It was hard to imagine that one day he'd be a grown adult who would leave home. In my heart, he would always be my little man.

Sunday afternoon, I packed my sketchbook and pencils in my satchel. "I'm off to see Mrs Cooper," I called out to Dad. Theo was over with Sam, as they did baking for the week to fill the biscuit tins for our lunches.

Stepping out of the cottage, I pulled my coat tighter around my torso as the wind caught the unbuttoned edge. Autumn developed a chill edge as the days shortened. With my head down and into the prevailing breeze, I increased my pace as I marched to my fortnightly afternoon tea with my patron.

After I rapped on the door, the maid showed me through to the conservatory. The glass structure was nestled against one side of the house and was protected from the prevalent wind. A round table sat among the lush shrubbery and palms. A lace-edged cloth draped over the surface. Mrs Cooper faced the open double doors, but her gaze seemed unfocused.

"Good afternoon, Mrs Cooper," I said. Clutching my satchel, I waited to be asked to sit.

She turned a wistful smile on me, as though she had been strolling through her memories. Today she wore a velvet print robe, edged with a silk fringe. It seemed a remnant of another era, like a wealthy bride might wear while lounging in her suite.

"Ah, Grace, punctual as usual." She gestured to the chair opposite her.

"I love your banyan. The pattern on the velvet is gorgeous." I placed my satchel by the chair I sat on, my gaze stayed on the cut and fit of the fancy dressing gown.

Mrs Cooper traced a fingertip along one sleeve where peacocks in lavish blues and greens were intertwined. "You find me in a nostalgic mood today. My George had this made as a wedding present. It's by Worth."

I sucked in a breath at the name of the legendary fashion house that rose to fame during the reign of Queen Victoria. House of Worth had dressed the wealthiest women across Europe. I wondered if I could ask to touch it, as to me it was a treasure to worship. "I should have known. The work is exquisite."

We chatted about her youth in England and the parties frequented by nobles and royalty alike. Which brought to mind a royal heading to our isolated corner of the world.

"Will you be travelling up to Auckland to greet the Prince of Wales when he arrives?" I asked as Mrs Cooper poured tea.

"Oh, no. He holds no novelty for me. Not when one has been presented to Queen Victoria. There was a formidable figure, despite her lack of stature." She passed the cup and saucer over, and her eyes misted as she recalled events in her youth. "Nor do I have any desire to curtsey any more than I have to. As I get older, I find I have grown rather fond of the looser attitude here in the antipodes. England is so strict, you are allocated a place in society and expected to toe the line and never step over it. My darling George was the fourth son of a viscount, and we were constantly reminded of our lower status. I rather like being patroness of Wellington society and leading them all, rather than being relegated to the end of the row." She sipped her tea and winked at me over the brim.

Conversation flowed as we moved from the upcoming royal visit to more recent and local events. I nibbled the porcelain of my cup to find the bravery to broach a particular subject. "When we spoke the other day, you mentioned that Mrs Taylor once had a beau, a Mr Russell Norton, who had simply vanished. Could you tell me more about him?" A wealthy man couldn't just vanish, surely?

"Intrigued by the mystery of it all?" Mrs Cooper selected a Vogue magazine from a pile on the chair next to her and placed it on the table.

"Yes. Especially given Mr Hammond's unfortunate end. Did anyone search Mr Norton's home to determine what might have happened to him?" Perhaps he lived alone and had suffered a heart attack while in the bath? But surely he would have had staff, or at the very least a cleaner, who would have discovered him eventually. My mind tried to conjure scenarios where a person could vanish with no one noticing. Something not too difficult for those who were alone or overlooked, but more difficult when you had money attached to your name.

"It wasn't a police matter, so no one ever investigated. Lynette thought he had given her the cold shoulder. His staff would have known if he had any sort of illness or accident and told Lynette when she called. Although that is the bit that was most odd. Lynette said that when she went to his home it was shut up and empty, and all his staff were gone as well." Mrs Cooper flicked through the pages and stopped at a spread that showed evening gowns for the wealthy socialite.

My attention was split. Part of me needed to delve into why Mr Norton disappeared and no one ever investigated. But my goodness, look at the beading on that chiffon! Fashion won, for the moment, and I dragged the magazine closer. "How marvellous. The beading echoes art deco designs."

"Don't doubt your abilities, my girl. I know you will have created something equally stunning for some lucky client to wear to the grand ball at Government House." Mrs Cooper selected another magazine and thumbed through the pages.

I glanced at my mentor. The gown I had crafted for her was elegant and, in my opinion, slightly ahead of fashion. Did she regret her choice now? "We could add beading to yours..." I made a half-hearted offer. Beading would clash with the lines of her dress, but I didn't want her to feel that her outfit wasn't as stunning in its own way.

"Oh, tosh!" She made an accompanying dismissive noise and wave of the hand. "We both know sparkly beads everywhere is not my style. Don't you dare place a single one on my gown."

Relief surged over me and swept away the anxiety. I gulped my tea to fill the space left behind. Only now did my mind circle back to Mrs Cooper's last comment about the disappearing Mr Norton. "If Mr Norton's house was empty of his staff, do you think he moved out in a hurry?"

"Ah. You think someone told him to move on *or else*? Like young Karl, who may be in the habit of penning angry threats to any man who sidles up close to his mother, and who might put their hand in her purse." The grand dame selected a scone from the plate in the middle of the table and sliced it in two, before spreading strawberry jam on each half. Next she added a dollop of cream, before gesturing for me to help myself.

My throat dried up as guilt crept up my gullet. Never a good liar. My thoughts must have been written all over my face.

"The police interviewed him about the note." Mrs Cooper bit off a corner of her scone and chewed.

"Oh?" I managed a non-committal noise as I selected a scone to accompany my tea.

Putting the savoury down, a smile tugged at her lips. "Karl confessed rather quickly and without any need for torture. I can only assume he decorated a desk somewhere in Europe and never developed any fortitude on the battlefield."

Or more likely Detective Archer asked the questions and his dark stare undid Karl as quickly as it did me. "So it is possible he wrote a similar note to Mr Norton, which resulted in his sudden departure."

"Possibly. The big question is whether Karl

followed through with his threat to Mr Hammond. He claims he never intended to do anything, and he was merely concerned about his mother's wellbeing. The whole affair has caused quite the rupture between mother and son. Not to mention that all of society is gossiping about her. Fools. Just because she found someone to make her smile and they don't approve of her choice." She let out a sigh and her attention wandered to the garden beyond the open doors.

My thoughts turned inward. Mr Norton might have been driven away or more permanently removed. Putting that mystery aside for later, how to prove just how far Karl Taylor would go to protect his inheritance? "Do you think he might have done it?" my voice dropped to a low murmur.

She ate more scone as she considered my question. Then took a slow sip of tea, before answering. "Despite his quick temper, I always thought him a rather cowardly sort. But one never knows what a man might be capable of, in a particular set of circumstances."

The scene played out in my head, as though I sat in the picture theatre. A confrontation. A heated argument. A weapon drawn in anger and thrust at a turned back. But whose hand was on the hilt? "What if Mr Taylor thought his mother had already found a replacement, one who most definitely had sights on her fortune? I wonder if he would be rash enough to boast of his ability to get rid of any beaus, or make such a threat again."

"You are thinking of dangling a piece of bait before

him and seeing if he snaps at it?" Mischief gleamed in the older woman's gaze.

"Yes." And I knew the perfect minnow to skewer on the hook—Harry.

"I'm sure that detective will uncover if Karl did away with the man who made his mother smile. Churlish, if you ask me, to deprive your mother of happiness and companionship in her autumn years."

"Did you ever consider re-marrying?" Curiosity about my mentor made me blurt the question out before I realised how impertinent it sounded. From what I knew, the couple never had children and Mrs Cooper lived alone. Apart from her staff, of course. Would I walk a similar path? Although without the grand house and staff to care for me.

Chapter Seventeen

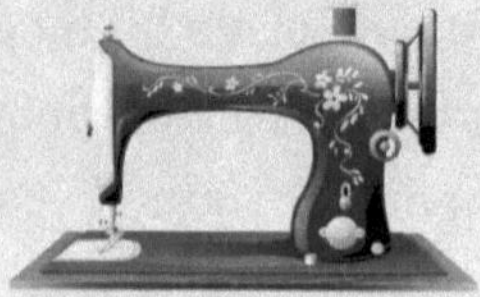

A SAD SMILE crossed Mrs Cooper's face. "No. Some loves burn so deep, they can never go cold. George is always here, with me." She tapped a finger over her heart, where a diamond cat with emerald eyes was pinned to the fabric. "Do not think this old lady is lonely, though. I have filled my life in many ways, and it has been a pleasure to encourage you to grow your business. You are not the only baby bird I have helped develop wings."

I finished my scone and the last of my tea. It did worry me that she might be lonely. Like Dad. Although he could never re-marry. For all we knew, my mother still lived. Somewhere. She hadn't wanted to be tied down with a child and never loved me enough to stay. So she simply up and left one day.

"What of you, Grace? Is there any beau who might sweep you off your feet? You didn't even have a chance to experience married life and are far too young to cloister yourself away like me." A mischievous sparkle lit her blue eyes.

Her words were similar to Frank's. I was no hypocrite and couldn't pretend any lifelong love for Freddie as Mr and Mrs Cooper had. Whatever I had felt for Freddie evaporated the day I realised he had been seeing another woman. Or possibly more. "I rather prefer my life as an independent business-woman. I'm not sure I want to hand over my finances to a man."

Mrs Cooper barked in laughter. "Good girl. Don't let any man take away what you have built. But you can still find someone to make your heart race."

Her words conjured to mind Detective Archer in a darkened alley, questioning me about my private life. That certainly made my heart race, although not in the way Mrs Cooper meant. I didn't like the way my senses all sprang to high alert around the policeman. It was exhausting to keep a rein on my nerves around him. Funny that I didn't immediately think of Frank when Mrs Cooper asked about romance.

"One day, perhaps. For now, my life is rather busy. My son turns five soon, and he is ever so excited about his birthday." I selected a small crustless sandwich from the tray and placed it on my plate.

Mrs Cooper plucked a blush pink macaroon from the tray and took a bite. "I am playing bridge with Lynnette this evening. If I see Karl lurking about in the library, I am happy to stir a little chum in the surrounding water to see if we can make him bite. I will have a quiet word to Lynnette, too. As much as I care for her, she needs to do something about that lad."

"Thank you, Mrs Cooper." I committed to a course of action without discussing it with either Sam or Harry. "If you see him, please tell Mr Taylor that Harry Sinclair, who has very expensive taste, is most besotted with Mrs Taylor and keen to replace Ricky."

At the end of my visit, I strolled back down the driveway in a thoughtful mood. Would Karl Taylor immediately dash off a note to Harry, or would he lie low now the police were asking questions about him?

As I stepped onto Tinakori Road, a familiar shape lounged against a motorcar. Frank pushed off the side of the Ford, angled his hat to stop the wind from sneaking under the brim, and approached me.

"You broke your promise, Gracie." As he tilted his head, sunlight lit his amber eyes and for a moment, they seemed to glow with suppressed anger.

I stood my ground, but my fingers tightened a little on the satchel. "Oh? What promise was that?"

"To stay away from the Scrum and Tackle." He fell into step beside me.

"I made no such promise. I said I wouldn't do anything foolish." My father had raised his eyebrows but hadn't made as much fuss as Frank.

"Getting caught there during a raid was foolish," he countered.

"The owner ordered a hundred pies from the Kostas Bakery. I was merely helping my friend deliver them. It wasn't like I was propping up the bar and clutching a pint of beer." The surge of anger strengthened my spine. I appreciated Frank's help, but he had no right to dictate my actions.

"Dwyer grabbed you," Frank spoke in a low, measured tone.

"Apparently he doesn't approve of women wearing trousers. As if I would take fashion advice from him." A shudder ran over me as I recalled the incident and the moment his fingers wrapped around my wrist.

"This isn't a joke. He's a nasty bugger and you're family. I always look out for my family," he bit the words out.

I let out a sigh. We were family. Just like me and Joseph. Lord, save me from overprotective men, even if their hearts were in the right place. "I certainly appreciate your warning...now."

"You don't turn your back on the likes of him. Not unless you have someone taller and more handsome behind you. Like me." He glanced at me and then returned his gaze to the stretch of road before us.

"I doubt I will ever encounter him again, and I certainly have no plans of returning to that pub. I shall stick to the Arms." I still struggled to picture smiling Ricky with such a hate-filled group. The former bakery employee had lived two such different lives. Or three, if I thought about his relationship with Mrs Taylor. Which life contained the truest version of Ricky?

Frank made a satisfied noise in his throat. "Good. How about a proper night out with me? You still haven't been to the Cricket at night, and I'd love to spin you around the dance floor."

I stopped in my tracks and made an impulse decision. "Yes. I would like that, Frank. Shall we say Thursday?"

He took my hand, drew me closer to him, and placed a quick kiss on my lips. "Thursday it is."

Monday was a wet and drizzly day and rain kept us from sitting outside to eat lunch, as we liked to do when possible. At midday, Etty and I took our lunch and headed upstairs to the new workspace. At least we could have a change of surroundings and a cup of tea while we ate our sandwiches.

We sat in the pristine workroom and discussed plans for the opening event. My assistant's excitement was as giddy as my own.

"Oh, Mrs Devine. I don't mind working longer hours, so we can make some special gowns to show. I even have a couple of friends who would love the chance to model, and they won't cost anywhere near as much as those fancy ones."

"That would be brilliant, Etty, if you could ask. We could make do with four, if they could each wear three gowns. We'd need their measurements, and they would have to practise how to walk and turn." My experience of fashion showings was limited to photographs in magazines. But I was sure Mrs Cooper would whip our models into something worthy of a Parisian atelier.

Then our conversation turned to other matters and my rather exciting Saturday night. "Sam and I were caught in a raid at the Scrum and Tackle. They were serving beer past six o'clock. I have to say being amongst that chaos and noise as men were arrested isn't an experience I want to repeat."

Etty screwed up her face. "My brother was there, too. The coppers took him away because he started swinging with his fists. Mum and I wish he would stay away from that place. He always gets in trouble with that lot. She says they came here from Ireland to keep us safe from all the strife over there. Then Patrick found a bad crowd to lead him astray."

"I might have served him without realising it." A pang of guilt brushed through me that I couldn't recognise my best, and only, worker's brother. Although I couldn't recall him ever coming to the shop. "Does he have red hair like you?"

She reached out and caught a tendril of bright auburn hair between her fingers. "Yes, and the short fuse that goes with it. I have talked to him about Constable Sullivan and his motorcycle. Silly lad screws up his face at the idea of hanging out with a copper, but I know he loves those contraptions, and he's dying to sit on one."

Reaching out, I patted her hand. "I am sure you will talk him around. Perhaps we could arrange a sort of *accidental* meeting to introduce Patrick to my cousin and his motorcycle?"

Etty warmed to that idea and rattled off numerous ways we could make sure Joseph and his favourite mode of transport were somewhere she and her brother could come across him. For my part, I was keen to throw Joseph and Etty together. A tingle deep in my stomach hinted that if I nurtured that seed, something beautiful might grow. Then an idea sparked.

"When I work late, my father usually sends Joseph to collect me on his horrid contraption. With this little collection and evening we are planning, I am afraid that you might also have to work some late nights beside me, Etty. Do you think your brother would come and walk you home?" I waggled my eyebrows in her direction.

Etty laughed, a clear ringing sound that filled the workroom with joy. "You are ever so cunning, Mrs Devine. Yes. I most definitely would require an escort home."

Our afternoon brought an unexpected visitor in the form of Mallory, Mrs Taylor's maid. In her early thirties, her brown hair pulled back in a severe bun and tucked under her hat. She clutched a parcel in her hands. "Hello, Mrs Devine. Mrs Taylor asked if you could have a look at her gown, please. Someone trod on the hem Saturday night and tore it and she's ever so upset. Said it's one of her favourites."

"Let's have a look at how bad it is," I said as Etty relieved the maid of the parcel and unwrapped the dress.

We spread out the blue silk on the cutting table. It was a gown I had made last year that had an asymmetrical drape at the back. Sure enough, some inconsiderate person had pierced the train with a pointed heel and created a tear about three inches in length.

I held my hand under the damaged fabric and considered how best to effect a repair. "It's so close to the hem. I could shorten it an inch and no one will ever know."

Mallory nodded. "Mrs Taylor said to leave it to your discretion, that she trusts you implicitly."

"If you pop back Wednesday, we will have it done." Lord knows when I would find the time, but I would put in the extra effort for one of my favourite clients.

"Thank you, Mrs Devine." She offered a shy smile that softened her features and then slipped from the shop.

That evening after work, I curled up in my friend's lounge with my feet under me and a cup of cocoa in my hands. This was my first opportunity to appraise Sam of my intention to use Harry to discover if Karl Taylor would dash off another angry note. "When I had afternoon tea with Mrs Cooper, we discussed Ricky and his involvement with Mrs Taylor."

Sam sat beside me, leaning on the rolled arm of the sofa. She stared directly at me with interest glinting in her dark eyes. "Did she have any salacious titbits to share?"

"No, it wasn't like that. I asked about Karl Taylor. Then she offered to have a quiet word with him, if she saw him while visiting last night." I took another sip of the cocoa and let the sweet but bitter taste swirl on my tongue for a moment before swallowing.

"And what word, in particular, was she going to share with him?" Sam lowered her drink and her eyes crinkled as she narrowed her gaze.

"Harry," I muttered over the rim of the cup. "I thought if perhaps Karl Taylor thinks Harry intends to fill Ricky's shoes, he might make a move against him. Then we would have more proof for the police."

Sam blew out a sigh. "I'll let Harry know. He had better move his desk in the library so his back is to a wall."

Since I was unburdening myself, I drew a breath and finished the tale of my Sunday afternoon. "I also said I would go to the Cricket with Frank on Thursday night. Do say you'll come too, so I don't do anything stupid?"

My friend gave me a hard glare that spoke volumes. Then she grinned, a wicked and mischievous thing. "I would love to be your third wheel. In fact, I shall drag Harry along and we'll make it a foursome. He'd love to dance with someone taller than him, like Frank."

We both burst out laughing. It was a bit mean to Frank when he thought it was a date with just the two of us, but I didn't trust my emotions around him.

Wednesday morning, I was cutting out a delicate piece of chiffon on the large table when the bell clanged like an alarm. Luckily, my nerves were like steel when holding my shears and tackling an expensive piece of fabric, otherwise, I would have cut a gash across the pale lilac expanse. Glancing up, a familiar and surly person entered the shop.

"Mr Taylor, what a surprise to see you here." Somehow, and somewhere deep inside me, I found a smile and a pleasant tone to address the entitled and selfish man.

"Mummy sent me to fetch some frock or other that you were supposed to fix. She treats me like an unpaid errand boy. I hope you don't expect me to pay you. I've not a penny on me." He paced the floor between the cutting table and the front window.

My smile nearly faltered. I struggled to think of a set of circumstances that would ever compel me to extend my hand to Karl Taylor and ask for money. Fortunately, Mrs Taylor was the perfect client who paid her invoices promptly and in the case of the repair work, in advance. "Yes. I have the dress and it is as good as new. There is no need to trouble yourself about payment. That matter is settled."

I fetched the box from the storeroom and peeked under the lid to double-check it was the blue silk. Then I carried the container to the counter and reached for a sheet of brown paper. Mr Taylor practically lunged and tugged the box from my hand.

"Don't bother about that. I can't wait while you add

silly wrapping." Without a care for the folded gown inside, he tucked the box sideways under his arm.

"I imagine Mrs Taylor wants to wear it to the show at the Cricket tomorrow night. You must be pleased to see your mother going out and finding some enjoyment in life," I called out as he turned to leave.

"What?" His feet halted, and a scowl crossed his face.

I rattled on and ignored his confused expression. "Harry is a lovely chap. So extravagant in everything he does. I never did understand how he affords his life-style, but he must come by the finances somehow."

Mr Taylor's scowl gouged deeper into his forehead. "I've not heard of Mummy having any new beau."

"I probably shouldn't have said anything." I placed a finger to my lips as though I swore him to secrecy. "But after Mr Hammond died and how terribly sad your mother has been, I thought it was lovely to see her smiling again. Don't you agree?"

"Who is this chap again?" His fingers tightened so hard on the box that one corner crumpled under his grip.

I grinned and kept up my bubbly performance. Which was rather impressive given my complete and utter inability to tell a pork pie in front of Detective Archer. "Harry Sinclair. I'm sure he will be the perfect gentleman and your mother will have a delightful evening. I wouldn't be surprised if he talks her into shouting drinks for the entire club."

Karl Taylor's right eye twitched, and he snorted

like a disgruntled horse. Then he stalked from my shop without another word and slammed the door so hard the bell jingled for a full five minutes.

"He's not a happy chap," Etty said.

"No. Apparently, he doesn't like *Mummy* seeing other men and possibly spending her own money." I stood staring out the window, wondering if Mr Taylor would take his unhappiness out on Harry.

Chapter Eighteen

THURSDAY EVENING, I took down my new frock from where it hung over my wardrobe door. Made of a light cotton in a sea green, it had a handkerchief hemline that brushed my calves. I swirled in front of the mirror, pleased with the effect. When I reached for the matching scarf that should have sat on my dressing table, my hand touched only the lace doily.

"Bother," I muttered. I had left it in the shop after a last-minute decision to add a fringe along the edge.

I had telephoned Frank earlier in the day and advised that I would meet him at the Cricket, as Sam would accompany me and we'd walk there. A silence had greeted that news, and I could imagine the displeasure on his handsome face at the addition to our party. My bravery deserted me before I told him Harry was also tagging along.

Downstairs, Sam waited for me. My friend was

smartly dressed in a light grey linen waistcoat over her white shirt, paired with wide-legged trousers in a darker grey. Her short dark hair framed her face in a style that made her look a little like Hollywood starlet ZaSu Pitts.

"You two look fancy." Dad peered over the top of his book. "Shame Joseph couldn't have joined you. That lad could do with a night out with other people, instead of spending it in the shed with his motorcycle."

"I know another bloke who spends rather a large amount of time in his shed." I kissed Dad's cheek before grabbing my clutch that matched my dress.

Dad huffed. "This fellow also knows how to chew the fat with a few friends a couple of times a week. I don't just oil my lathe, you know."

If only Etty could talk her brother into spending some time with the quiet constable, then Joseph would have other people in his life. And not just Etty's brother. "Joseph said he was working tonight, so at least he won't be alone this evening."

Dad stared at Sam. "Have a good night, and be careful."

Since Mr Kostas had succumbed to the influenza, Dad had extended his paternal duties to include Sam. Just as Mrs Kostas had been an amazing surrogate mother for me, Dad now repaid the favour by issuing sage advice. Like, be careful. None of us wanted to see Sam hurt, and it was a mixed blessing that the attacks had all targeted men. So far.

Sam shoved her hands deeper into her pockets. "I am who I am, Mr Sullivan. I'll not pretend to be anything else just to make small-minded bigots feel comfortable."

"I would never ask you to change, Sam. Just keep your eyes peeled for trouble, and get out if something starts," Dad said.

She saluted and tugged me out the door.

"Dad means well. And I am sure he worries about both of us in equal measure," I muttered as we hurried around the side of the cottage and along the road.

Sam blew out a sigh. "I know. But sometimes it grates that people think I can't look after myself."

I hugged her arm tighter. "Let's not find out, please." Talk of fighting or having to defend yourself made me nervous. "Where are we meeting Harry?"

"He's going to wait outside the club. Doesn't want to go in alone. The attacks are making us all nervous," Sam said.

We crossed the road and headed along The Terrace, discussing what to serve for Theo's birthday party as we walked. When we neared Plimmer Steps, I pulled Sam to a halt.

"I need to call in at the shop. I left my scarf there." I gestured down the steps and the pale light from the lamps at either end.

"I'll come with you." Sam made to follow me.

"No. You go on." I waved her away. "I'd rather not leave Harry alone outside the club. While I'm in the shop, I'm going to leave a note for Etty. If we are late home tonight, I suspect she will be in before me tomorrow morning."

Sam laughed, and it erased her worry. "All right. But don't be too long, or we'll have to come find you."

It took me fifteen minutes to unlock the shop, find where I had left the scarf, and leave instructions for Etty. Then I locked the door again, tugged on it to make sure, and carried on my way. There were plenty of people about, and I joined the back of a crowd, so I wasn't walking alone.

With each step, a jaunty mood bubbled up inside me. Tonight, I would dance with Frank, laugh with my friends, and for a few hours pretend to be a twenty-five-year-old woman without a care in the world. The autumn air seemed sweet, and I didn't mind the chill that washed over my skin as fast dancing would soon chase that away. As I passed a coffee shop, a familiar figure sat at a small table tucked under the eave of the building. Yet there seemed an air of despondency about the usually vibrant person. Even her coat was a dull navy and seemed to blend with the shadows gathering around her.

"Mrs Taylor?" My voice held a hint of uncertainty.

She looked up from her contemplation of the steam rising off her coffee. "Good evening, Mrs Devine."

I curled my fingers at the end of my scarf and approached her table. "I wanted to apologise. I never intended for my actions to cause you any distress. When I found that note in the hamster cage, I had to turn it over to the police, and I had no idea who had penned it." The apology tumbled from my lips.

She gestured to the chair beside her. "Sit for a moment, if you would. I find myself somewhat of an outcast these days and would relish a little company."

I dropped to the indicated seat, my attention drifting inside the cafe for a moment where a group of four women, who appeared to be well dressed and in their fifties, stared in our direction and whispered amongst themselves.

Seeing what drew my attention, Mrs Taylor shook her head and picked up her coffee cup. "I did see you at Richard's funeral, but silly pride made me deny it. I don't blame you for events, Mrs Devine. You did what was right. It was foolish of me to think no one would ever find out. Now all of Wellington gossips about me, chattering of the sad old woman carrying on with a man younger than her son."

A hand clenched around my heart. I never suspected that putting together the shredded note would hold her up to the ridicule of gossip. "You are an eligible woman with much to offer, and Mr Hammond made you happy. Not that any of it is their business."

Her shoulders heaved in a sigh. The light that usually shone from her dimmed like a lamp wick trimmed low. Twice now she had bravely ventured into a relationship only for odd circumstances to whisk the gentleman away.

"He did indeed make me happy. And I like to think that I was a steadying influence on him, or that he had some enjoyment from our brief association." Her eyes were unfocused as she wandered through halls of memory in her mind.

"I enjoy our association, and you are one of my favourite clients. I am sorry I cannot say the most favourite, but that spot was claimed by Mrs Cooper some years ago. But you are my number two." I placed my clutch on my lap and rested my hands over it.

A smile flitted across her face. "That is lovely of you to say, Mrs Devine, but I am sure you have any number of fashionable and thin young things you prefer to clothe."

"No." I blurted the denial, perhaps a little too hastily. "I have clients who, yes, have model-like figures. But the gowns I design look the same on the dress form as they do when being worn by them. You, on the other hand, bring my designs to life. You breathe a vibrancy into fabric and stitches that none of them can match. You gift clothing a type of magic that so many lack. That is why you are one of my favourites. It always takes my breath away to see you wearing one of my designs."

Her eyes misted with tears. "Thank you. Richard said he was drawn by my vibrancy and never saw my age or shape. I think that was why I...well, it doesn't matter now. Do you have any children?"

"Yes, one. Theodore. He will turn five soon." A burst of love shot through me on saying Theo's name and my mind conjured his face before me.

"I am sure that, like me, you dote upon your son.

Karl was a cherubic little boy and how I spoiled him. I wanted to give him the world and now, as a grown man, he demands the moon and the stars to accompany it." The wistful smile that had appeared for a moment drooped at the corners.

"We want what is best for our children." I would have given Theo the world if I could. While he might lack in toys, or new clothes, or a fancy garden to play in, my son had an abundance of love.

"Yes. You understand. Temperance told me that we should make Karl believe I had found another paramour already. He was in a terrible mood this afternoon and we had quite the argument. That is why you find me here. Do you really think he did it?" Her gaze cleared. Tears were driven away by the thought that spoiling her son as a child had created a man capable of murder.

"I don't know. All I know is that a life was lost, and someone should be held accountable for their actions." We were short on suspects, and Joseph hadn't shared who else they pursued in the case.

She nodded and sipped her coffee. "Oh, poor Richard. He told me he wanted to be a better person and that he had done some terrible things in his old life. He wouldn't tell me what he had got up to. I assume the usual antics of young people. A bit of vandalism, or perhaps he stole a motorcar."

I held my tongue. Ricky had been caught up in something much darker than the normal larks that bored youths engaged in. "I think it says much that you encouraged him to find a new path."

She flashed me a quick smile. "I did try. At his core, he was a kind man and simply needed a little guidance and a nudge in the right direction. Whatever he had done, it preyed on him. Why, it was only that terrible week that I had told him to write it all down. The act of putting on paper what he had done would be a sort of confession. That very evening, he sat at my desk and poured his worries onto several pages. Then he folded the sheets into an envelope and sealed it. He asked me to keep it safe until he decided who best to hand it to."

"He wrote out an accounting of what he had been involved in?" Hope crept through my torso that at least one crime, or a series of crimes, might be solved and the culprits brought to justice.

She traced a fingertip around the rim of her empty cup. "So he said. I think getting it out like that was just the action he needed to take, to finally turn his back on that group and make amends."

Turn his back. Make amends. You don't betray your team. Don't you have a relative in the police?

Fireworks erupted in my brain. "Mrs Taylor, I think I know exactly who Ricky wanted to hand that envelope to—my cousin. He is a constable. Could I collect it from you tomorrow morning, and pass it on?"

"Of course. It will bring me some measure of peace, to know his soul will rest easier knowing it was given to the right person." She pushed the cup and saucer away.

"Thank you, Mrs Taylor! Ricky can still make amends from beyond the grave, and perhaps someone else will be held accountable for taking his life." Clutching my little handleless bag, I stood, said goodbye, and took off along the street as fast as dignity and the pedestrians would allow. Soon, I turned into the side street, illuminated by the twinkling lights strung along the outside of the Cricket. Inside, I left my coat, hat, and gloves with the attendant. The ticket for my items I shoved into my clutch for safekeeping. Then I pushed into the main floor to search for Frank and my friends.

The first person I spotted was Frank. That was the advantage of being tall—he was a landmark in any setting. He stood conversing with a group of men on one side of the curved bar. One gentleman I recognised, was Liam Fleet, the owner of the Cricket. The stage was occupied by musicians and a woman clutched the microphone and sang a familiar tune that rippled over my skin and made me hum along.

The Cricket skirted the alcohol rules by donning the disguise of a dance school during the day. The women who performed at night ran classes during daylight hours for eager young girls. At night, it claimed a unique status as a private establishment which never sold alcohol after six. Instead, patrons hired glasses, which came filled with the liquid of their choice.

As I tried to decide if I approached Frank or not, I spotted Sam and Harry with their heads bent together at a booth towards the back corner. My course veered close to Frank, his head turned, and he raised a hand in my direction. I smiled and held up my clutch, indicating I would deposit my bag at our table. What I really wanted to do was tell Sam about Ricky's confession and speculate what it might contain.

"I was starting to get worried. What took you so long?" Sam said as I approached the table.

I deposited my clutch on the table to free up my hands. "I saw Mrs Taylor sitting outside a cafe and had a quick chat...about Ricky. Karl, her son, is rather angry at the idea that Harry here already has designs on her bank account."

"Sam advised me that I am cast in the role of bait. I shall sit here with my back pressed to the bench all night." Harry laughed, but it had a nervous, brittle edge.

Sam's eyes widened, and she slid along the velvet-covered bench seat, making room for me to sit. But just then, a warm hand pressed to my waist.

"You look beautiful tonight, Gracie," Frank murmured in my ear.

I turned and took hold of his hand. "Thank you, Frank. You look dashing, as always."

Frank had removed his jacket, exposing his lean frame in the fitted waistcoat, and rolled up his shirt sleeves to his elbows. He managed to look handsome and slightly reckless, with his disregard for the unspoken dress code that required gentlemen to wear a jacket at all times.

"You owe me a dance and I have come to collect."

Frank stepped backwards, pulling me towards the dance floor.

The singer had moved off the stage for a break, and the musicians played a fast song suitable for a fox trot.

I glanced at Sam. I needed to tell her all I had learned in the last fifteen minutes, but I found myself swept away in Frank's arms. The matter could wait for one dance. Or maybe two.

Chapter Nineteen

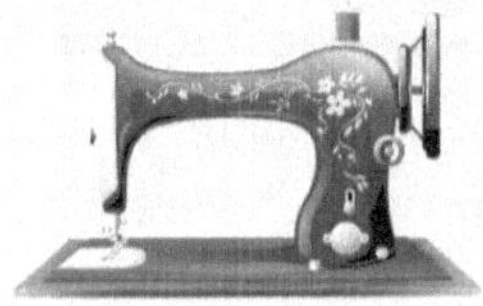

FRANK KEPT hold of me for three dances. The first dance reminded me of all I was missing out on by sitting at home with cocoa and a book. Frank led strongly, and I had nothing to do but let my body respond to the music. I still enjoyed the second dance, but worries nibbled at the edges of my mind like mice attacking the skirting boards. By the third dance, I was peering around Frank, trying to spot Sam and Harry.

"You are supposed to be here with me," Frank said as he spun me around.

"I am sorry, Frank. Recent events have me a bit on edge, and there's something I need to discuss with my friends." My fingers tightened in the soft cotton of his sleeve as I scanned the revellers and tried to find my friends. Which was no easy feat in the dim lighting, and when Sam lacked in height. She could have been obscured by anybody.

A flash of auburn hair caught my eye and underneath it, a familiar shaped face. It had to be Etty's younger brother—Patrick Doyle. I wondered what he was doing here, but perhaps it was good that he hadn't returned to the Scrum and Tackle. The crowd at the Cricket was less prone to arguments or police raids.

The band finished the song, and Frank stopped so abruptly that I nearly tumbled into him. He stared down at me. "Sort your business, and I'll deal with mine. Then I intend to claim you for the rest of the night."

His words raised the hairs along my arms. I wasn't sure I wanted to be *claimed*. That sounded like something you did to a library book. But I found a smile for my son's beloved uncle. "Give me half an hour, Frank. You know what we women are like once we get chatting." I made a joke of it to soothe any hurt he felt.

It must have worked. He appeared mollified and kissed my cheek, before striding off to find whoever he intended to do business with in the shadowy corners of the club. I hurried back to our booth, only to find it devoid of my friends. My clutch was buried under a jacket and a few half-empty glasses littered the tabletop.

I grabbed my bag, made from the leftover scraps from my dress, and tucked it under my arm. Then I set off to find Sam. I prowled the edges of the dance floor, but none of the people swaying to the slower tune were my nattily dressed friend. Nor did she seem to be huddled in a booth talking to someone else. That left one place...the bar.

The bar curved in a gentle arch, giving the staff a half-moon shape to work inside. Towards one end, I spied Sam and let loose a sigh of relief. My friend was deep in conversation with someone on her right. I slid between her and the patron on the left, muttering an apology when I bumped his elbow. With a gentle touch, I tapped on Sam's arm.

She turned with a scowl on her forehead, as though she had expected someone else. The dark look dropped away and relief washed over her features. "Oh, it's you. Finally."

"Sorry. Frank can be rather insistent. Where's Harry?" I peered along the row propping up the bar, but none were the dapper librarian.

"He's off chatting to some chap who wanted to know how to enrol in the university." She waved a hand to the other side of the club.

"We're supposed to be watching him." Had we missed Karl Taylor pulling Harry out for an argument over his mother?

"It seemed harmless enough, and it wasn't Taylor. Harry can't get into trouble explaining the arcane paperwork needed to become a student." Sam took a sip of her drink and tapped her toe as the singer came back onto the stage to belt out *You Ain't Heard Nothing Yet* by Al Jolson.

Before I found myself humming along to the tune, I asked, "Who was it? Anyone we know?"

Sam peered around the club, as though trying to refresh her memory by spotting the librarian and would-be university student. "Young chap with red hair."

So far that evening, I had only seen one red-headed man in the crowd. "Was it Patrick Doyle?"

Sam screwed up her face. "I think Harry called him Patrick. I got the impression they had met before. Why?"

Fear surged up my throat. Patrick was the lad who idolised the Bin Men. The hate group that had sent Ricky, unsuccessfully, to target Harry.

"I think our bait has caught the wrong fish. We have to find them. Now!" I pushed off the bar and scanned the revellers around us.

Sam's hand slipped into mine. "They won't be out on the floor. Too public. Harry's like an owl and avoids the light. Let's check the booths and dark corners."

Before anxiety overwhelmed me, I closed my eyes and forced my mind to replay the moment when I was dancing with Frank and had noticed the Irish man. What direction had he been taking? Opening my eyes, I pointed with my free hand. "There. They were headed that way."

I tugged Sam through the press of people. Beside the other end of the bar, and away from the tables and booths was a clear space. And a doorway.

"I think that's the toilets. Harry has far more class than that," Sam protested.

"That's not what they are doing." I pushed open the door and pulled her through.

Beyond was a short corridor. One side led to the

ladies' powder room and men's toilets. The other short branch ended in a solid door. One that my dad would quip was built to withstand an angry kicking. Grabbing the handle, I turned and flung it open.

The darkened alleyway ran between the Cricket and the next building, giving access to the rear for a man pushing a trolley, but too narrow for a motor vehicle. The single bulb over the exterior door struggled to reach the shadows. From somewhere farther along came muffled noises.

"Harry!" We both rushed towards the sounds.

At the end of the alley, and with the light behind us, we made out six shapes standing in a close circle like a miniature Stonehenge. A fiery glint from one could only be the red hair that ran in Etty's family. Laughter erupted as one of the men kicked at something on the ground. A shape like a dropped sack of grain curled into itself and groaned.

Sam turned to me and pushed me back towards the Cricket. "Go back and get help!" Then she flung herself at the closest man.

Run away? I snorted. I would never leave my friends alone with a bunch of thugs. Regardless of my own safety, I tossed my clutch to the ground and then shoved a solid back as hard as I could.

The man stumbled forward and called out. "There's more of them."

"They'll go down as easily as this pudding," a gruff voice called out.

Sam swung her arm and punched one man before ducking under his return hit.

As my eyes adjusted to the dim light, the horrid scenario became clearer. Harry lay on the ground, curled on himself. I only recognised two of his attackers. The short and broad mass of Geoff Dwyer and the lighter frame of my assistant's brother.

I pointed a finger at Patrick, who was bouncing on his toes beside Geoff. "I will be telling your sister, Patrick Doyle."

That made his feet go flat and still. He glared at me. "How do you know Etty, then?"

"I'm her employer. Although given your behaviour, perhaps not for long." A shape lunged for me, and I yelped and jumped sideways.

Patrick sucked in a breath. Perhaps it was finally dripping into his brain that not only was he in a whole lot of trouble, but his actions could cost his sister her job. Not that I would ever sack Etty over something an empty-headed sibling did, but a little fear might put him on a straighter road.

I tried to find Sam in the dark but couldn't spot her behind the wall of brawn. Nor could I reach Harry to help him. I needed to do something. Like turn their attention to me and make a bigger ruckus so they momentarily forgot my friends.

"You're a coward, Geoff Dwyer," I shouted at the top of my lungs, hoping someone on Willis Street might hear, even as fear skittered along my skin.

He laughed. "No one calls me a coward and gets

away with it. At least you look like a girl, not like that other one. Grab her, Patrick."

I kept moving around them, hoping to distract them from Harry, who seemed awfully still and quiet. "You're a double-sized coward. You need a gang to attack a man on his own, and you're the sort of chicken who stabs a former friend in the back."

"Don't know what you're talking about you daft bint," Geoff growled the words, but there was a note of hesitancy in his voice. He swiped an arm through the air, missing me.

Pieces had come together in my mind and now I stood my ground. With hands planted on my hips, I found the courage to face him. "You killed Ricky. Not your usual style to use a knife, or was it because you're not as strong as you make out?"

The others fell silent. Then one ventured, "It was you that did Ricky in?"

"She's mad. I know how to shut her up." Geoff shoved me, and I tumbled backwards. Flinging out my hands, I scraped my palms on the rough ground as I broke my fall.

"You leave my friend alone." Sam rushed in front of me, drew back her arm, and there was a loud smack as she struck the former rugby player in the face.

Dwyer roared and threw a hit at Sam. "Get her! We'll take out two pieces of trash tonight, lads."

Sam stumbled backwards and nearly tumbled over me. Two of the men grabbed hold of her shoulders. She struggled in their grasp, trying to wrench free as Dwyer advanced on her.

I hurried to my feet, kicking my brain into action. Ricky had been about to go to the police, to unburden himself. Geoff must have caught wind of it, which was why they argued on the steamer. As events of that day unfurled in my mind, I saw the angry Geoff confronting Ricky as he lounged by the wharf. Their argument had turned fatal.

I kept talking. "If you thought to silence Ricky, you're a bigger fool than you look. He wrote it all down, you know. A full confession of all your horrid acts, naming every single one of you. You're all going to jail for what you have done." I had no idea if that was true or not. For all I knew, Ricky could have written a fulsome apology to his flatmate for keeping him awake at night or for his taste in music.

But my words struck harder than any punch.

The men paused, then muttered amongst themselves. Quiet doubts were magnified by the dark.

"Maybe we should stop, Geoff. This has all gone too far, and it's not a lark anymore." Patrick's voice came from somewhere behind me.

"None of you leaves unless I say you can. We only have one rule—you don't betray your team! That rat Hammond got what he deserved. Snitches get stitches," Dwyer yelled. He pulled something from behind his back that made a faint rasping sound. Light glinted on metal as he raised his arm, a knife clutched in his hand.

In that instant, I understood what it must be like to

face a rugby player intent on tackling you to get the ball. Although in this case it was one wielding a weapon. Dwyer surged in my direction. I cringed, waiting for the cruel slice of the same blade that stole Ricky's life.

But some force grabbed Dwyer by the collar, spun him around by the arm clutching the knife, and punched him square in the jaw.

Detective Archer.

The detective delivered a rapid series of blows. A clatter came as the knife flew from Dwyer's fingers. Then the policeman threw an uppercut that saw Dwyer stumble back. His head hit the brick and the whites of his eyes glowed before he slid down the wall to puddle in the alleyway.

Whistles sounded and heavy footsteps ran down the alley towards us, with truncheons raised and torches that illuminated the packed earth and surrounding brick walls. Since the lads in uniform had the vigilante group occupied, Sam and I rushed to Harry. Kneeling at his side, I lifted his head to check if he was breathing. I tugged free my scarf and pressed it to a gash on the side of Harry's head.

Detective Archer shook out his fist and flexed his fingers. Then he turned to me and gestured at Harry. "How is he?"

The fallen librarian muttered something indistinguishable but possibly about late return fees on a book. "He's conscious and worried about an overdue library book."

A tall policeman stepped forward. Joseph was among the men who had rescued us.

"Search the ground. You'll find a knife that will most likely match that used to kill Richard Hammond. Put all of this lot in cuffs and load them in the wagon." Then Detective Archer indicated Harry, who was now moaning about his favourite tie being ruined. "This one needs to go to the hospital."

"The ambulance is not far away." Joseph cast me a worried look. "Are you all right, Grace?"

"Me, yes. My dress, however, will never recover from the amount of blood on it. Sam came to my defence with a cracking right hook." I smiled at my friend, kneeling beside me. She would have a black eye in the morning from the blow Dwyer landed but didn't appear to have any other injuries.

She grinned. "Never pick a fight with a baker. We're used to pounding dough."

The thugs who were brave when facing one lone librarian, turned subdued in the hands of the numerous policemen. Soon, all six were handcuffed and marched down the alley to the waiting paddy wagon.

I left Harry's side to tap Joseph on the shoulder. "Go easy on Patrick Doyle. He's the brother of my assistant, Etty. She says he's a good lad, caught up with a bad crowd. He needs better role models and, I understand, has quite a keen interest in motorcycles."

A range of emotions flitted across Joseph's face in the low light. "He'll be charged with the others. But I'll have a word to the detective about him."

Standing on tiptoes, I placed a kiss on my cousin's cheek. "Thank you, Joseph. And I'm sure Etty will be grateful, too."

My cousin ducked his head. Did he blush? It was hard to tell in the dark with the torches pointing in different directions. I would have much to tell my assistant in the morning.

Chapter Twenty

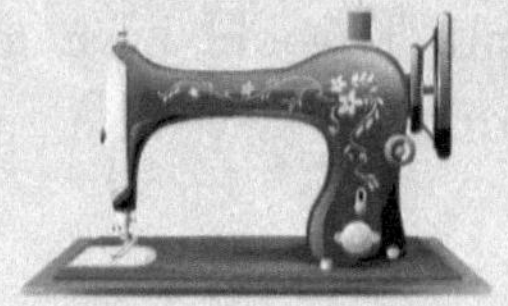

WE WATCHED Harry get loaded into the ambulance and it rattled away. I worried that the sway of the vehicle would cause further damage to him, but the staff assured us they would look after him and that we would be allowed to visit in the morning.

Sam rubbed her knuckles and stared at the detective with a narrowed gaze. "I suppose you came in use, at the end."

I ignored my friend who bristled at the detective's presence.

"Did you know about the thugs luring men out to attack them?" I asked, omitting mention of the irrational fear that fuelled the beatings.

Detective Archer watched the ambulance turn a corner, then spoke. "About a year ago I started hearing stories of bar brawls that didn't seem...right."

"Aren't all fights wrong?" I found myself drawn closer to him, even in the face of Sam's anger. On this occasion, I had nothing to confess and wanted to know how the police arrived in time to arrest the group.

He turned, and his eyes sparkled in the low light. "When two fellows argue, it can spill out to the road. In those instances, we have numerous witnesses. People love to report such fights and often take one side or the other." His smile faded. "But these fights weren't spill-over. There were no reports of arguments escalating. No one noticed anything amiss. The men seemed to wander outside of their own accord, only to be ambushed."

"These were never fair fights," Sam all but growled.

The Bin Men—cleaning up the streets and taking out the trash. To my mind, it was a disgusting way to refer to a group of people who others thought had no right to go about their lives like everyone else.

"No." The detective agreed with Sam. "Six fellows to one is not a fair fight, especially when the one has been lured out by someone he thought he trusted."

"Harry thought he was explaining the university enrolment process to a prospective student," I murmured. There would be an awkward conversation with Etty tomorrow about her brother's involvement, but I hoped his arrest would lead to a change in his behaviour.

"The problem I faced was that no one would file a report. Nor would those beaten up tell us what was really going on. Even the lads who ended up in hospital, like Mr Sinclair." He gestured off in the direction that Harry and the ambulance had been taken. "Then came the whisper that one of the gang was going to spill all. That he'd had enough and was going to name names. It was the break we needed to stop the attacks."

"Ricky. He had realised what they were doing was wrong. He wanted to make amends so that he could start a new life. But Geoff Dwyer obviously heard the same whispers. He was on the steamer that morning and confronted Ricky about it." I nearly let slip what I had seen in the moment that Ricky's skin touched mine. *Remember what we do to traitors.* "Ricky did make his confession, in a way. He wrote everything down and gave it to someone he trusted for safekeeping."

Detective Archer took a step closer to me, and I congratulated myself on not fleeing in the opposite direction. "Would you happen to know who?"

I inhaled and caught a scent that reminded me of filtered sunlight through trees and sun-warmed earth. "I am to collect it from that person in the morning. I promised I would turn it over. Ricky asked if my cousin was a policeman, and I believe he intended to talk to Joseph."

"Found it, sir." A policeman interrupted us. From one gloved hand, he dangled a knife.

Detective Archer shook out a handkerchief and took the blade. "A trench knife. Quite a distinctive piece with odd markings on the hilt. Good work, constable. This should prove a key piece of evidence."

"Even if one of the lads had spoken about what happened, what would the police have done, anyway?

None of you care about us." Sam's words were clipped, like a challenge.

The detective turned to face Sam. "*I* care. Everyone has the right to live in peace. At least now Dwyer will be put away, but if people had trusted me, we might have caught him before anyone else had been hurt. Or killed."

"I don't think Ricky was such a loss anyway," Sam muttered.

"Samantha Kostas!" I glared at my friend. You didn't speak ill of the dead.

"It's true. He would have lured Harry out for a beating, just like that Patrick did." She crossed her hands over her chest.

"No. You're wrong. I think Ricky *did* like Harry but pushed him away to keep him from the attention of the others. So he could say their informant was wrong about the librarian. We all make foolish decisions that we regret later on. Shouldn't we be given the chance to grow and reflect on what we should have done differently?"

Sam huffed, but I knew she would come around to my point of view. In the end, Ricky had saved Harry— by not luring him into a darkened street weeks earlier. I was saddened for Mrs Taylor, who once again lost a companion who made her smile, but perhaps someone else would come along to brighten her days.

"An excellent point, Mrs Devine. To err is human, to forgive...divine." A hint of humour simmered in the detective's reference to my married name.

"That's Grace, always giving people a second chance, even to those who don't deserve them." Sam threaded her arm through mine.

The detective's dark gaze considered me for a moment, then he said, "If you ladies are unhurt, I shall return to headquarters and make a start on my paperwork. I shall collect the letter from you tomorrow, Mrs Devine."

"Of course," I murmured.

He touched the brim of his hat and walked back to the road and his waiting policeman.

Sam and I followed at a slower pace. "Shall we splurge on a ride home? I don't fancy walking tonight," she said.

"Yes. I've had rather enough heart-racing excitement for tonight," I replied.

The next morning, I first called at Mrs Taylor's home and collected the letter Ricky had written. Then I carried on to the shop, where Etty enveloped me in an enormous hug.

"Oh, Mrs Devine! I'm so glad you're not hurt. That idiot brother of mine has done it this time. Da is ever so angry and has said that Patrick either straightens up, or he's going to be shipped to family in Australia. *Australia!*" she repeated the word and her tone dripped with horror.

To be fair, I shared her dismay at the idea. Australia

was where England had sent her criminals. The country seemed inhospitable, the climate in some parts was either terribly hot or wet, and most of the middle bit was desert. Then there were innumerable animals, insects, and plant life out to kill or maim. I had heard stories of spiders bigger than your hand. A shiver ran over me as I recalled Dad's tales.

Etty let me go.

I shrugged off my coat and hung it on the hook by the door. Then I placed my handbag under the counter and fetched my apron. "Perhaps last night will prove to be a turning point for Patrick. He did try to stop things and told Geoff Dwyer it had all gone too far."

When I turned around, Etty was wringing her hands in her apron, and her bottom lip quivered. Before I could tell her not to worry too much about her brother, her eyes glistened with unshed tears.

"I'll understand if you want me to leave your employ because of what happened," her voice broke over the words and a single tear spilled free.

"Fire you?" I sounded as horrified at the idea as she did at the mention of Australia. "I have no intention of letting you go, Etty, because of your brother's foolishness. In fact, I was planning on promoting you to my second when we move upstairs and hire the new girls."

"Really?" She fossicked in a pocket for a hanky and blew her nose.

"Really. Although, you could torture your brother a bit with the idea that he had lost you your job if you think it will make him more compliant." I winked.

Etty grinned and then hiccupped in relief. "You are the best boss, Mrs Devine."

I grinned. Normally I would disagree, but today I basked in the compliment.

We set to work, and it was just before lunchtime when I glanced up as the door opened soundlessly, and Detective Archer slid into the shop.

My stomach lurched. His mere presence set up a disconcerting push-pull reaction inside me, as neither body nor mind could decide if he was friend or foe. Even more unsettling was the idea that my senses might finally resolve that he was a friend. Then what?

"Hello, Detective Archer. I have the letter for you." I jabbed a pin into the cushion on my wrist and fetched the fat envelope from my bag.

He took the letter from my fingers and tapped it against his palm. "Thank you. Hopefully, this will strengthen our case against Dwyer. Going back over my notes of the day Mr Hammond died, we had two reports of a man showing off a distinctive trench knife. Witness reports place both Dwyer and the knife at the scene. The coroner will confirm today if his was the weapon used, as he found rather an unusual pattern around the entry wound. Many a man occupied his hours by personalising his trench knife during the war, Dwyer's work will seal his fate."

Sadness filled me for the life taken. "At least there will be justice, and these terrible attacks will stop. I do have another question, if you are able to answer it, Detective?"

He tucked the letter in his jacket pocket, then he took off his hat and instead of placing it on the cutting table, as had become his custom, he spun it in his hands. "If I can."

"Mrs Taylor was seeing a gentleman called Russell Norton, who suddenly disappeared. Did he also meet foul play?" I worried for my client who had such rotten luck in love. Surely there was a decent older man who could return the smile to her face?

Detective Archer's full lips quirked. "I did enquire as to his fate and can reassure you that he is alive and well. His wife demanded that he return to their home in Christchurch, or he would face legal proceedings. He acquiesced, rather than face divorce."

"Oh." Relief that the man hadn't been murdered butted up against a surge of anger. Perhaps it was as well that Mr Norton left in such a hurry. He didn't deserve Mrs Taylor after all.

"There is one more thing. I wanted to apologise to you."

"For what?" For the life of me, I couldn't think what he was apologising for. Only the night before he and his men had come to our rescue, and possibly saved Harry from critical injury. Unless he wanted to make amends for not getting to the alley sooner.

"When we met at the Scrum and Tackle, my questions were...uncalled for." His fingers tightened on the dark grey felt, and I found myself mesmerised by how they flicked the hat brim.

"You were doing your job, Detective. And a most

thorough one at that." Now kindly keep your nose out of my private business, I wanted to add.

"A job I took too far. I am most sorry if I caused you any distress." There was an openness in his expression as he caught my gaze and the sincerity of his apology caught in my throat.

"Apology accepted. Although after how you saved us all last night, perhaps we could say we are even." Mentally, I congratulated myself that so far in our conversation I hadn't grabbed hold of anything that could be considered a murder weapon. "Could I ask you another question?"

He dropped his hat and rested one hand on the cutting table. "Of course."

"How did you know to be in that alley, at that time?" For the detective and his men to be so close at hand, they had to have some sort of tip-off.

"Let's just say a little birdie told me." We both reached for his fedora at the same time, and his warm skin skimmed over mine.

The same odd memory that was no memory surged over me.

The elderly Maori woman beamed with a warmth that made me smile in return. This time, she stood in a garden overflowing with flowers. Fat bumblebees droned from one bloom to another. Lush, deep red plums and apples hung from trees. A fantail sat on her shoulder and chatted in her ear. I wanted to rush towards her, but something held me back. On seeing my hesitation, she waved a hand at me and said in a clear voice, 'Hāere mai ki konei!'

The image wavered and disappeared before I could ask what the phrase meant.

"Are you quite all right, Mrs Devine? You might be experiencing some shock from last night." Detective Archer fanned me with his hat.

"Yes. Just a little tired. I'm not used to such exciting evenings." It wasn't until we got home the previous evening that I realised I hadn't seen Frank before we left. He probably scarpered when he heard the police whistles. Did he even spare a thought for where I was, his family? But he was a problem to worry about later.

"Why don't I make a cup of tea, Mrs Devine?" Etty said, glaring at the policeman for causing me any distress.

"I shall leave you in the capable hands of your assistant." Detective Archer placed the fedora on his head and gave it a tap. "Until next time, Mrs Devine."

Somehow...I didn't doubt there would be a next time.

In book 3, Grace is drawn into a conspiracy to harm the Prince of Wales...

GATHER THE ANARCHISTS

This royal visit is going to off with a bang...

Edward, the Prince of Wales, is about to step foot on Kiwi soil and Grace is frantically finishing gowns for her wealthy clients to wear at the balls thrown in his honour. But then a horrible accident and a dying man's last moments, draws her into a conspiracy to harm the prince.

As Grace follows the strands of a last memory, she discovers there is a patchwork of conspirators all with grudges against England and the royal family. This plot has unravelled larger than her group of friends and if she's going to hem in the anarchists and save the prince, she needs help. There's only one person she can turn to...Detective Archer.

Can Grace discard her differences to confide in the policeman with their common goal of saving the prince, or will there be an explosive end to the royal visit?

BUY: GATHER THE ANARCHISTS

https://tillywallace.com/books/grace-designs-mysteries/gather-the-anarchists/

Author's Historical Notes

Days Bay is a residential area in Lower Hutt in the Wellington Region of the North Island of New Zealand. It is walled on three sides by steep bush-clad slopes. The area proved so popular that on the city side of the harbour, large wharf gates (since removed) had to be put up to control the crowds, as well as barricades. The Wellington Harbour Board built a special Ferry Wharf (finished by autumn 1897) as the swarms of day trippers created real difficulties at the Queens Wharf. Neither newspaper reports of shark fins spotted in the water, nor infestations of venomous katipō spiders in rotten wood on Days Bay's high tide mark could deter all the beachgoers. Donkey rides began on the beach in 1910. It also once held a water slide that was the longest in the southern hemisphere, having been built for an exhibition. But it was sadly dismantled in 1912, as I would have loved to incorporate it in this story!

The Days Bay Pavilion was an ornate wooden late-Victorian structure, providing teas on its deep verandahs, a restaurant, evening dances and outdoor concerts. It was highly popular until it was totally destroyed by fire in October 1952.

Drivers who use The Rigi as a shortcut from Northland to Glenmore Street would be surprised to know that in the 19th century coaches used to wend their way up the steep road. In the days before the Kelburn viaduct (the old one was built in 1900 and its replacement in 1931) the main commuter route to Karori was a tortuous journey up The Rigi and over the hill where Karori Tunnel is now. The Rigi is largely a one-way street these days, except for the stretch at the bottom below the intersection with Governor Road.

It has existed since the 1850s and was referred to as The Rigi after the Swiss mountain of the same name. Though in the early years, the street was called Old Karori Road, gradually The Rigi became more formally adopted. For many years the dominant buildings in The Rigi were the St Vincent de Paul school and church on the right coming down. The Catholic Church bought the site in 1916 and had the church and school built soon after.

The Presbyterian St John's church has been serving Wellington city for a hundred and eighty years now. The original wooden church burned down in 1884 and a much grander and larger one that sits on the spot today was designed by renowned architect Thomas Turnbull.

Victoria University was founded in 1897. Originally lectures were held in rented accommodation while a permanent place was found for them. In 1906, the university moved into the purpose-built Hunter Building in its new home of Kelburn. By the early 1920s, the role had risen to some 700 students.

A trench knife was a weapon used during the war for close combat—such as in the trenches. During the Great War, soldiers customised these weapons as they were not standard issue. Sometimes they were improvised from bayonets, and they often contained distinctive markings or modifications that made one weapon identifiable as belonging to a particular soldier.

Also by Tilly Wallace

For the most complete and up to date list of books, please visit:

https://tillywallacebooks.com

Available series:

Tournament of Shadows

Manner and Monsters

Highland Wolves

Grace Designs Mysteries

About the Author

Tilly drinks entirely too much coffee and is obsessed with hats. When not scouring vintage stores for her next chapeau purchase, she writes whimsical historical fantasy novels, set in a bygone time where magic is real. With a quirky and loveable cast, her books combine vintage magic and gentle humour.

Through loyal friendships, her characters discover that in an uncertain world, the strongest family is the one you create.

Email: tilly@tillywallace.com
Web: https://www.tillywallace.com
STORE: https://www.tillywallacebooks.com

facebook.com/tillywallaceauthor

bookbub.com/authors/tilly-wallace

goodreads.com/tillywallace

instagram.com/tillywallaceauthor